AS BLACK
AS EBONY

AS BLACK
AS EBONY

SALLA
SIMUKKA

Translated from the Finnish by **Owen F. Witesman**

HOT
KEY
BOOKS

First published in Great Britain in 2015 by Hot Key Books
Northburgh House, 10 Northburgh Street, London EC1V 0AT

Original edition published in Finnish by Tammi Publishers in 2014
Hot Key Books edition published by agreement with Tammi Publishers and
Elina Ahlback Literary Agency, Helsinki, Finland

A CIP catalogue record for this book is available from the British Library.

ISBN: 978-1-4714-0310-1

1

This book is typeset in 10.5 Berling LT Std using Atomik ePublisher
Printed and bound by Clays Ltd, St Ives Plc

www.hotkeybooks.com

Hot Key Books is part of the Bonnier Publishing Group
www.bonnierpublishing.com

ALSO BY SALLA SIMUKKA

As Red As Blood
As White As Snow

For everyone who loves. For everyone who is alone.

I've been watching you.

I've been watching you when you didn't know. I've been watching every move you make and every expression of your face. You thought you were invisible and unremarkable, but I have seen everything you do.

I know you better than anyone else. I know you better than you know yourself.

I know everything about you.

FRIDAY, 8 DECEMBER

1

Lumikki awoke to a gaze.

A gaze aglow with warmth. It was hot, burning her skin and mind. The eyes were as familiar to Lumikki as her own. Pale blue, the hue of ice and water and sky and light. Right now the eyes were smiling, although the gaze was steady and firm. A hand rose to stroke her hair and then continued in a light caress along the line of her cheek to her neck. Lumikki felt a shudder of desire, first in her belly and then below. Its grasp was so strong that she wasn't sure whether it felt dizzyingly good or agonizingly painful. She was ready in a second. Blaze could have done anything to her. She was open to everything, absolutely everything. She trusted Blaze and knew that anything he did would be pure pleasure. They made each other feel good because they only wanted the best for each other. Nothing less would do.

Blaze held his hand lightly on her neck and continued his gaze. Lumikki could already feel herself throbbing. Her breathing sped up. Her pulse pounded against Blaze's fingers. Leaning in, Blaze grazed her lips with his, drawing his tongue teasingly along her lower lip, not kissing in earnest yet. Lumikki had to work hard to stop herself from grabbing Blaze with both hands and sucking his lips greedily. Finally Blaze pressed his lips gently against Lumikki's mouth and began to kiss her as irresistibly as he could. Lumikki would have groaned if she could have made any sound. She closed her eyes and thought of abandoning herself without restraint.

Suddenly the kissing changed, becoming softer, tender, more tentative. It wasn't Blaze kissing her any more. Lumikki opened her eyes, and the person kissing her drew away slightly. Lumikki looked him straight in the eyes.

Brown, friendly, happy eyes.

Sampsa's eyes.

'Good morning, Sleeping Beauty,' Sampsa said and bent down to kiss Lumikki again.

'How old is that joke now?' Lumikki muttered as she stretched out her arms, which felt numb.

'At least a hundred years.'

Sampsa's laughter buzzed on Lumikki's neck. It tickled. It felt nice.

'Actually, it's much older than that. Perrault wrote down his version in the 1600s and the Grimms did theirs in the 1800s. But the story was being told a long time before then. Did you know that in one of the older versions the Prince didn't wake Sleeping Beauty with a gentle kiss at all? He just raped her. And even that didn't wake her up until she gave birth to twins who . . .'

Sampsa had slipped his hand under the blanket and was caressing Lumikki's thighs, gradually moving towards her crotch. Lumikki was starting to have a hard time talking. The desire her dream had awoken was still present.

'Save the lectures for school,' Sampsa whispered and then kissed her more demandingly.

4

Lumikki stopped thinking about anything but Sampsa's lips and fingers. She had no reason to think of anything – or anyone – else.

Sitting at the kitchen table, Lumikki looked at Sampsa's back as he brewed her espresso in a Moka Express and heated water for cocoa on another burner for himself. Sampsa had a nicely muscled, confident back. His plaid flannel pyjama bottoms hung just low enough on his hips to show the two depressions between his buttocks and lower back. Lumikki resisted the urge to go and press her thumbs into them.

Sampsa's dark-brown hair was mussed, and he was humming a song that his group were practising. They played modern folk music, and Sampsa was the group's violinist and vocal soloist. Lumikki had heard them play a couple of times at school assemblies. Not exactly her kind of music, but it was fast, happy and energetic. For their genre, they were obviously quite good.

Early-December sleet splashed against the kitchen windowpanes. Lumikki pulled her feet up onto her chair, wrapping her arms around them and resting her chin on her knees. At what point had it become perfectly normal to have a sweet, half-naked boy bustling about in the kitchen of her pathetic little studio apartment every morning?

She supposed it had all started at the beginning of the autumn term, in mid-August. Maybe not right at the beginning, since for the first few days everyone in the school had wanted to talk to Lumikki about the house fire in Prague and hear how she had saved the cult members inside it from committing suicide. How did it feel to be a hero? How did it feel to be famous? How did it feel to see her picture in all the magazines? Of course

5

the media in Finland had covered the story, and practically every newspaper wanted to interview Lumikki when she got home. But she declined.

To her inquisitive schoolmates' questions, Lumikki had responded briefly, until they became bored with how little they were getting out of her.

Then Sampsa came. He had been at the same school as Lumikki all along. Walked the same halls, sat in the same classrooms. Lumikki had known his name, but Sampsa had never been anything more than another face in the crowd.

One day Sampsa came and sat down next to Lumikki in the cafeteria. He came to chat before class and then walked home with her as far as the square downtown. And he did it all as if it were the most natural thing in the world. Sampsa didn't pressure her or force himself into her life. Whenever he realised that a casual conversation had reached its natural conclusion, he didn't try to drag it out. He never took offence at Lumikki's occasional, rather unfriendly rebuffs. Sampsa simply talked to her, looking at her with that friendly, open gaze of his, being present but knowing when to leave before the mood became awkward.

Sampsa's every action said: 'I don't expect anything from you. I don't hope for anything from you. I don't demand anything from you. You can be exactly how you are. I just think it's nice to spend time with you. My self-respect doesn't depend on you smiling at me, but I wouldn't mind at all if you did.'

Gradually Lumikki found herself looking forward to seeing Sampsa. She felt warm when he sat next to her and looked her straight in the eyes, sincerely and happily. Tiny butterflies began flitting in Lumikki's stomach when Sampsa's hand grazed hers.

They started meeting outside of school. To go on long walks together, to drink coffee together, to go to concerts together. Lumikki felt as if she were a feather carried by a gentle breeze into moments and situations that felt utterly natural and right. Walking hand in hand with Sampsa. The slightly fumbling yet warm first kiss one dark November evening. The hand that stroked her hair and back the first time he slept at her place. Sampsa was patient. He didn't try to lead Lumikki into doing anything she wasn't ready for.

Then, one night, Lumikki was ready. And she wasn't the slightest bit surprised that physical intimacy with Sampsa felt just as good and safe and right as everything else with him.

By December they were an official couple. Lumikki felt like things were the way they were supposed to be. She had finally fallen in love with someone new. She had got over Blaze and their break-up, even though it had taken a long time – more than a year. Blaze had disappeared completely from Lumikki's life when his gender reassignment process from physical girl to physical boy was at its most difficult. Blaze thought that he couldn't be with anyone then, not even his beloved Lumikki. Lumikki had been left with no option other than to accept Blaze's decision, even though she could never completely understand it.

But now Sampsa was in her kitchen, brewing coffee and humming and generally making Lumikki want to kiss every vertebra of his spine.

This was life. Life was good.

It didn't even matter that the sleet was now buffeting the window so hard it almost sounded as if someone was clawing at the glass, trying to get in.

7

2

Once upon a time there was a key.

The key was metal, perfectly palm sized. On its head was a skilfully cast image of a heart. The key was forged in 1898. The same year a small chest was made, with a lock that fitted the key. Over the decades the surface of the key was burnished by the touch of human hands. The first person who held it was the metal smith who forged it. Then it made its way to the hand of the first owner of the chest. He had seven children, all of whom held the key in turn. At that point, the key had been touched so many times that identifying individual fingerprints was impossible.

The last time the key was touched was more than fifteen years ago. Then two people held it, several times in turn. In their hands, the key felt much heavier than it weighed. And when they turned the key in the lock of the chest, they felt as if someone had twisted a sharp, serrated knife in their hearts. The last time the key was touched, salty tears fell on it.

Then the key was hidden. And it lay hidden, alone, abandoned year after year.

But it was not forgotten. In the world there were two people who thought of the key every day. It was branded onto their minds and still burned like glowing iron. If their thoughts could have made the key shine, its scintillating light would have revealed its hiding place from miles away.

Once upon a time there was a key that was hidden.

In stories, like in real life, everything hidden wants eventually to be found.

The key waited to be touched again and to open the chest. The key waited patiently, immobile and mute.

Soon its time would come.

3

This was Lumikki's forest. The branches were black shadows; the black shadows were branches. Tree roots coiled along the ground like snakes before diving underground to form a wide, thick network. They curled around each other, the veins of different trees uniting beneath the soil, drinking from the same life force. The branches traced their own map between the trees and towards the sky, with so many lines that light struggled to find a route through. The branches were arms, brush strokes and hair. Some thin, some delicate. Some thick, some strong. All beautiful.

The forest was a game of shadows, a dance of dim light and mist, hushed whispers and sighs, passing currents of air that made the hair on her arms stand on end. All of the shadow creatures, dream animals, sneaking beasts and darkness dwellers bade Lumikki welcome. She was with her kind again.

The blackness settled around and inside Lumikki, at once familiar and foreign. She ran more freely in the forest. She breathed deeper. The ribbons holding her hair came undone and her plaits fell out as the sylvan wind seized them, doing with her hair what it would. Twigs and leaves clung to her locks. The fabric of Lumikki's silk dress ripped. She scratched her arms. She smelled the soil and decomposing leaves. Lumikki's eyes focused, and she saw the smallest movements of the shadows. There was blood on her hands, drying quickly and turning black. Trying to wash it away would be futile. It would stay on her hands always, because Lumikki was a killer, a predator.

This was Lumikki's forest. In its darkness there was room for passion and fear, despair and joy. The air that filled her lungs was heady. In the embrace of the forest she grew into something whole. She became more than herself, more free. Lumikki settled down to lie on the ground, pressing her palm against the damp earth and wishing that she could become part of the roots, merging with them and penetrating the earth to find the heart spring.

The forest sighed and throbbed around Lumikki as if it had one single pulse. Her pulse.

'OK, good! That bit about the heart is a perfect way to end the scene.'

Tinka's voice snapped Lumikki out of whatever state she had been in and she sat up on the stage. She felt like she had just woken up from a deep sleep. This scene in the play always affected her that way. She got so into it that for a moment she forgot she was on the stage of the small auditorium in their school rehearsing a play. They were calling it *The Black Apple*.

Lumikki still wasn't sure whether agreeing to act in the play had been a good idea. Sampsa was the one who had lured her into it.

11

'Hey, it's a new take on *Snow White*. With a name like yours, how could you pass that up? The Snow White role could have been written for you,' Sampsa had said, smiling that happy, encouraging smile that Lumikki was ready to do just about anything to see.

At least she had been ready to take a part in a play, although the thought of playing her kinda-sorta namesake felt a bit self-aggrandising. It was bad enough that half the people she met felt compelled to make dumb jokes about her fairy-tale first name. Tinka, who had written the play and was also directing it, only needed a couple of rehearsals to convince Lumikki that the script was actually pretty great and the production was going to be fantastic. Tinka had just started at their school that autumn, but she had enough chutzpah to direct students two years older than her.

On the outside Tinka was a stereotypical artsy student, with her eclectic, constantly changing clothing and hairstyles. One day she might come to school in a tutu with red hair coiled in a bun, the next day in boots, holey jeans and an oversized hoody with her hair in a rat's nest and the day after in a three-piece suit and a bowler. Variety and fickleness weren't an attempt to get attention for Tinka, though, and she wasn't putting on an act. She was direct, down-to-earth and determined in a way that Lumikki admired.

The Black Apple opened with the Prince gazing at Snow White lying in her glass casket, burning with love for the beautiful, motionless maid. Then they began transporting the casket to the Prince's castle, and on the way one of the bearers tripped, jostling the casket, which dislodged the piece

12

of poisoned apple in Snow White's throat, allowing her to wake again. So up to this point the plot followed the classic fairy tale. However, in Tinka's play, when Snow White awoke from her poison coma, she wasn't thrilled about her role as the Prince's bride-to-be. She was used to the forest, to its shadows and beasts. She didn't want to move to a golden castle to have servants wait on her hand and foot. A queen had too little freedom to do as she pleased. The Prince only worshipped her beauty and wasn't interested in Snow White's mind.

Tinka's play had strong feminist overtones, but it wasn't preachy or didactic. It was just intense and disturbing. None of the characters in *The Black Apple* were purely virtuous. Not even the Huntsman, who did try to save Snow White but was motivated by his own desires and aspirations, too.

Sense by sense, Lumikki returned to the ordinary, real world surrounding her. Recovering from the last act always took some time. It was a powerful, hypnotic scene: Lumikki would remain lying on the ground. The lights would go dark. For a moment the stage and auditorium would be in perfect blackness, with the sound of a beating heart echoing increasingly loudly over the auditorium speakers. Just before this Lumikki had learned of the Huntsman's death and killed the Prince with a sharp silver hair comb. Then she had fled the castle back to her beloved forest, to the company of the darkness and shadows and beasts.

When they rehearsed the scene for the first time with all the props, sound effects and lighting, no one had been able to say a word for a long time afterwards. They just glanced at each other, as if asking, 'Did you feel that, too? Were we just somewhere else?'

'Next run-through on Monday night. Same time, same place!' Tinka reminded them.

'Aren't we about ready now? How about we take a night off?' suggested Aleksi, who was playing the Prince.

Tinka cast him a deprecating glance.

'We have two weeks until opening night and a ton of work left to do. And some people still need to learn their lines all the way through.'

Aleksi shrugged and started marching out of the auditorium.

Sampsa came over to Lumikki and stroked her back.

'You were really good. Again.'

'Thanks,' Lumikki replied as she tied the laces of her combat boots.

Her hands were still trembling slightly.

'See you tomorrow. I've gotta run. I'm already late and my mum's going to have a fit.'

Sampsa kissed Lumikki's forehead, threw his backpack over his shoulder and left. The last couple of scenes had given him time to change out of his Huntsman costume already. His family had a tradition of gathering for dinner every Friday night, including Sampsa's grandparents and an aunt who lived in Tampere. They had been doing it for years, so Sampsa didn't feel like he could make exceptions and skip it occasionally. He had invited Lumikki to come a couple of times, but so far she had declined. The thought of the way everyone would stare as they sized her up was unpleasant. Lumikki had promised to come for coffee on Sunday, though, when only Sampsa's parents and little sister would be home. That was already a high enough hurdle for her.

The dark, deserted school lay in a drowsy silence as Lumikki and Tinka walked down the stairs to the mirrored foyer. The halls looked strange when they were empty, and their steps echoed. During the day the corridors were crammed with students and the decibel level exceeded industrial safety limits.

Tinka was analysing the problems with each scene of the play, but Lumikki couldn't concentrate on what she was saying. Had agreeing to act in the play been a mistake? She didn't like how completely immersed she became in her role and how the real world disappeared around her. She wasn't acting Snow White running through the forest. She *was* Snow White running through the forest, feeling and smelling the blood on her hands. Snow White's pulse was Lumikki's pulse. Lumikki wasn't used to that kind of loss of self-control, and it frightened her.

Eventually Tinka noticed Lumikki's detachment, and they donned their coats in silence. Around her neck Lumikki wrapped the heavy red wool scarf her former classmate Elisa had made for her and sent in the mail. They still kept in touch. Last winter Lumikki could never have guessed that Elisa would become a true friend to her.

Outside it was snowing large, fluffy flakes that melted the instant they touched the black ground. No hope yet that December would turn out white.

'Some of the cast might still be out to lunch, but at least you aren't. You're killing it,' Tinka said as they walked through the school gates.

Then she waved and turned in the opposite direction from Lumikki, who didn't manage to get out anything sensible in reply. Mud squelched under Lumikki's boots as she continued towards the city centre. Further along the footpath, she saw the school psychology teacher and one of the maths teachers, who had apparently been working late, too. This time of year the teachers tended to work long hours marking tests and essays. Some of them preferred not to take their work home, instead staying at school late into the evening. In a way it was funny seeing them outside of school, chatting and laughing together. Even so, Lumikki was happy to be far enough behind them not to be able to make out any of their words. She thought it was best to know as little as possible about her teachers' private lives.

The illuminated red-brick tower of the Alexander Church rose into the sky, stately and familiar. It was so dark that the few old gravestones in the churchyard were invisible from the footpath. The large snowflakes looked like feathers against the black branches of the trees, fallen from the wings of angels. Lumikki pushed her hands deeper into her coat pockets and walked faster.

In her left pocket something strange rustled – something that didn't belong there. Lumikki pulled it out. It was a white sheet of paper folded four times. Lumikki opened it fold by fold. It was a short letter written on a computer. She stopped under a street lamp to read it.

My Lumikki,

Your prince doesn't know you. Not in the play and not in real life. He only sees your outer shell. He only sees a part of you. I see deeper, into your soul.

16

You have blood on your hands, Lumikki. You know it. I know it.

I see every move you make.

You will hear from me again soon. But know this: if you tell anyone about my messages, one single person, there will soon be much more blood. Then no one will survive the opening night of your play.

With love,

Your admirer, your Shadow

Lumikki's breathing intensified and she looked up from the letter. Something flickered at the edge of her field of vision. Something black.

But when she looked towards it, she saw nothing but the long, dreary shadows of the trees.

Alla kvällar lät prinsessan smeka sig.
  Men den som smeker stillar blott sin egen hunger
  och hennes längtan var en skygg mimosa,
  en storögd saga inför verkligheten.
  Nya smekningar fyllde hennes hjärta med bitter sötma
  och hennes kropp med is, men hennes hjärta ville ännu mer.
  Prinsessan kände kroppar, men hon sökte hjärtan;
  hon hade aldrig sett ett annat hjärta än sitt eget.

  (Every evening the Princess allowed herself to be caressed.
  But the caresser only satisfied his own hunger,
  while her desire was a shy mimosa,
  a wide-eyed fairy tale in the face of reality.
  New caresses filled her heart with a bitter flush
  and her body with ice, but her heart wanted more.
  The Princess knew bodies, but she sought for hearts;
  she had never seen any heart but her own.)

Lumikki read 'The Princess' quietly to herself. The words calmed her. She had read her copy of Edith Södergran's posthumously released collection *The Land Which Is Not* so many times she basically knew every poem by heart. Or at least the first words always brought back the rest of the lines. Familiar poems were like mantras. Their calming effect rested on the way the words flowed one after another in just the right order, without any surprises or change.

Lumikki couldn't go straight home after reading the letter, so she headed for the library. Was someone really following her every step? She tried to rationalise away the fear. In all likelihood, the letter was just a joke. Black humour. A cruel game. Someone somewhere was laughing right now thinking about how frightened she would be, but they would soon jump out and reveal the truth. Gotcha!

But what if the letter was real? What if she really did have a crazy stalker who was prepared to kill? Lumikki couldn't risk treating the letter too cavalierly. Her life experience had left her with little doubt that people were capable of evil deeds. She had endured years of brutal school bullying and then seen up close the ruthlessness of the international drug trade. Just that summer in Prague she had seen a charismatic leader use fear to manipulate his religious cult into attempting mass suicide.

All her life was missing was a deranged stalker, Lumikki thought with a bitter snort.

The sounds around her were pleasantly muffled. Calm footsteps, the rustling of pages, hushed conversations with words not quite audible. Lumikki knew that if she moved to the base of one of the arches that made up the vaulted ceiling of the Tampere City Library, she would be able to hear every word that was being said at the base of the same arch on the other side of the room, otherwise out of earshot. The architects Reima and Raila Pietilä had designed it that way. However, Lumikki didn't want to hear anyone else's private conversations right now. She wanted to be wrapped in the protective familiarity of the sounds of the library, surrounded by people but still alone, so that she could calm down and build up the courage to go home. The library was only a two-minute walk from the Alexander Church.

Lumikki had always found the dome and the avian plume of arches of the undulating building soothing inside and out. There was just enough walking space between the shelves, but if you wanted you could hide in them. The library was full of round reading tables and secret nooks where no one ever bothered you.

Lumikki wanted to text Sampsa and ask him to come over for the night after his family dinner. No matter how late that would be. But she had never done something like that before, so Sampsa might wonder why. And then Lumikki would have to lie, and she didn't want to lie to Sampsa.

No, she would have to endure this night alone. Then she would have to find out as soon as possible who put the letter in her pocket. She would have to do that alone, too.

Lumikki had thought she would no longer be as alone as she was before. She had thought wrong. Suddenly she felt that familiar emptiness and desolation filling her inside. She was always alone, in the end. Lumikki stared at the stanzas of the poem, unable to read any more.

Just then a deep, crisp scent of pine forest surrounded her and a warm hand gently brushed her neck.

'Edith Södergran. Are you reading our poems without me?'

Lumikki knew before she turned to look over her shoulder. She knew before the voice and the words. She knew from his smell and his touch.

Blaze.

He stood sideways behind Lumikki. Smiling. Real. He looked maybe a little more like a boy than eighteen months earlier. His hair was shorter and lighter, and there was a new calm and self-assurance in his posture, but otherwise he looked exactly the same. Those ice-blue eyes were the same, and Lumikki sank into them instantly, as if breaking through a frozen crust as thin as thought and plunging into the black lake beneath.

A storm of emotions washed over Lumikki. She wanted to curl up in Blaze's arms, as close to him as she could be, and tell him everything about the letter and how afraid she was and what had happened in the past year and all the longing and loneliness and dreams and black thoughts and ask him to protect her and save her from solitude and evil and take him home and tear off all his clothes and her own and get tangled up with him on the hallway floor and kiss and kiss and kiss and press every hungry inch of her skin against him and burst into flames and forget herself and the world and that they were two different beings because front to front they were one, as seamless as could be with no boundaries, and Lumikki wanted to burn and burn and burn without fearing the fire for once.

Lumikki swallowed. A tremble ran through her. She couldn't say anything.

21

'It's nice to see you. Wanna go for coffee? Or are you busy?' Blaze asked, as if it were perfectly natural to chat like normal people.

'No,' Lumikki managed to say.

'Good. Should we go upstairs to the café?'

'No. I mean, we can't go for coffee.' Blaze stared at Lumikki, a little confused, but then he smiled mischievously.

'We can do something else if you want.'

With trembling hands, Lumikki put her book back on the shelf and pulled her knitted cap down over her ears.

'No, we can't. I'm busy. I can't see you. Not now.' Lumikki heard the words coming out of her mouth, haltingly, breathlessly.

'OK. Well, some other time, then. Is your phone number the same? I'll call or text you.' Blaze's voice was warm and composed.

Don't, Lumikki should have said. That was what she wanted to say. But she also didn't.

'I have to go. Bye.'

Lumikki's legs wanted to run out of the library, as fast and as far as possible away from Blaze. But she forced herself to walk. Briskly and purposefully. Without looking back.

Not until she was outside in the fresh air did Lumikki realise she should have said she was dating someone.

She hadn't said it, though, because after diving into the burning ice water of Blaze's eyes, she had forgotten that fact completely.

I love you.

Three words that are so easy to say, but so hard to mean. I mean them. I breathe each word and they become a part of me. I say them to you and they become a part of you. My love moves into you. It makes you burn even more beautiful, strong and radiant.

I make you brighter than the brightest star of the night-time sky.

You become mine, completely. As was always meant to be. Because it is your fate. And mine.

SATURDAY, 9 DECEMBER

5

Sister, sister, sister, sister.

The word pounded in Lumikki's head, as it always did now when she was visiting her parents in Riihimäki. It would just never come out of her mouth. Her mum had made chèvre lasagne for lunch, which was one of Lumikki's favourites, but today she could barely taste it. Lumikki felt as if all her pleasure centres had been numbed. Food was just necessary fuel. Even coffee didn't taste good.

Lumikki guessed it was because of the letter. She was still convinced that it was just a practical joke at her expense, but the message still bothered her, lurking somewhere behind her thoughts. It made colours duller and covered the world in a thin haze. If Lumikki could just figure out who the letter was from, she would get her revenge, which would be civilised but definitely served cold.

But at her parents' house, the only thing Lumikki could think about was how she still hadn't discovered whether she really used to have a sister. The memories awakened during the summer in Prague, which Lenka had triggered with her lie, had felt so real. She had been so sure that she had once had a sister. Since returning to Finland she wasn't so sure, though. She had thought she would just slap the question down on the table as soon as she got home, but that hadn't happened.

When Lumikki had told her mum and dad about Lenka, she had left out the part about her claiming to be Lumikki's sister. Over the autumn Lumikki had exchanged a few emails with Lenka, who had started studying maths, chemistry and biology independently, hoping eventually to get into medical school. Lenka had also subtly let Lumikki know that she had never moved out of Jiří's apartment. Jiří had found a new job at a local paper. Lumikki had read between the lines that after saving Lenka from the burning building with Lumikki, Jiří had found he liked taking care of Lenka. Lumikki was happy for them.

Sometimes Lenka signed her emails 'your sister in spirit'. Sister was the word that filled Lumikki's thoughts. But she avoided saying it out loud.

Why? Wouldn't it have been easiest just to talk about it? Lumikki didn't know what was holding her back.

Maybe it was something in her mum and dad's concern and earnestness, all the warmth and love they had shown since she returned from Prague. The uncharacteristic intimacy. The idea of interrogating them just felt wrong. Her dad's trip to Prague years ago had turned out to be just a coincidence, without any connection to the sister issue at all, so Lumikki hadn't grilled them about that either.

To tell the truth, she had enjoyed all the warmth. She hadn't wanted to jeopardise it by talking about something that might only have been her imagination anyway. People could invent memories if they really wanted to or if they thought that something had happened in the past.

Days without bringing it up had turned into weeks, and weeks had turned into months. Eventually Lumikki had realised that there wasn't any natural way to bring up the topic any more. Her parents' burst of tenderness had subsided, and all three of them had returned to their old, familiar roles, where they talked about general things, kept in touch just as much as was necessary for it to seem normal and tried to avoid awkward lulls in conversation – like the ones a Saturday lunch like this had so much potential for.

'Would you like some more?' her mother asked, to fill one such pause.

'No, thank you,' Lumikki replied. 'Could I look at some of those old pictures, though?'

'Again?' her dad asked. 'We only have the ones you've already seen.'

'Yeah, but I've been thinking that I might be able to use them for a project at school,' Lumikki explained.

'I'm going to make the coffee,' her mother said, beginning to clear the plates just a little too hastily.

Lumikki sat with the photo album on the living-room sofa, slowly turning the pages. She knew every picture by heart. She had looked at them so many times, this autumn especially. She had tried to find some solution in them, some key.

There was mum and dad's wedding picture. Some pictures from a cottage in Åland. A couple of fuzzy pictures of their home in Turku where they had lived until Lumikki was four. She had only dim memories of the house. It was an idyllic two-storey wooden house in the Port Arthur area. Very different to this stubby row house in Riihimäki. It felt strange that they had moved into a house that was so much cheaper. For the price of their place in Turku they should have been able to buy a big new house here. Apparently there were money matters no one ever told Lumikki about, too.

'Why did we move here from Turku?' Lumikki asked. Looking up from reading his paper, her father furrowed his brow.

'For work.'

That seemed like a strange explanation. Her father had always worked on the road, and most of his trips took him to Helsinki. And you would have thought library jobs for her mother would have been easier to find in a big city like Turku than a tiny berg like Riihimäki. Lumikki didn't press the matter, though.

She wondered yet again why there were so few pictures. There were just a couple from each year of her life, and most of them weren't very good. Not that Lumikki needed hundreds of baby pictures like people took nowadays, starting at the actual birth, but how few there were was still strange. Lumikki had seen childhood photo albums at other people's houses and they were always much thicker, and there was usually more than one. Maybe her mum and dad had just never been very interested in photography. Or maybe they hadn't been interested in taking pictures of Lumikki.

At one picture Lumikki paused longer than the others. In it she was seven years old. She stood in the middle of a schoolyard. It was winter. She remembered Mum suddenly wanting to take a picture after dropping her off at school.

'Come on, smile!' her mum had said.

In the picture Lumikki stared seriously, straight at the camera, without the slightest hint of a smile. She simply didn't have any reason to grin in that place. The bullying had started that winter, and Lumikki had hated every day she had to go to school. Now she looked at the picture and saw the chilling fear behind her defiant gaze.

Lumikki never wanted her eyes to look that way again. But she knew she saw it all too often in the mirror, even now.

Lumikki closed the album. It wasn't going to tell her anything new today. It wasn't going to reveal the secrets hidden in the past.

After coffee, her mother asked Lumikki, 'Are you going to stay for a sauna tonight?'

The question was more rhetorical than a real invitation. It was the question you were supposed to ask.

'No. School work,' Lumikki replied.

Just as she was expected to reply.

Walking to the railway station, Lumikki passed her old middle school. Seeing the building and the yard always made her taste iron in her mouth. Those had been the worst years of the violence and humiliation. The hitting and shouting. The isolation. All the lies to get Lumikki to come to school at the wrong time, to bring the wrong PE clothes, to do the wrong homework. She had tried to be careful and only believe what she had heard with her own ears from the teachers, but she had still been tricked time and time again. It was easy to forge messages and get other kids to play along.

Just as nauseating was the memory of how she had finally risen up against her bullies, Anna-Sofia and Vanessa, brutally attacking them.

The rage. The loss of control. The hunger to kill.

Afterwards, Lumikki didn't know whether she was more afraid of the bullies or of herself. Of everything she knew she was capable of and how it felt to want to take another person's life just to put an end to her personal hell. Lumikki wasn't proud of her feelings, but she also didn't try to deny experiencing them. That was why she had tried so hard to teach herself composure and self-control. She didn't intend to give other people the upper hand, but she also didn't want to act in anger.

At least, Lumikki *tried* to have that be her guiding rule. Following it wasn't always so easy.

Sunny memories of Riihimäki were few and far between for Lumikki. One of them was of the Riihimäki Theatre where she had seen a play when she was nine. She couldn't remember any more what the play was, but that didn't matter. Lumikki had loved the smell of the auditorium, the hush that replaced the hum of conversation in the audience and the moment when the lights had dimmed but the performance had not yet begun. The sense of tension and expectation when everything was still possible.

Lumikki had sat right in the front row, obliging her to tilt back her head to see properly. The actors had been almost close enough to touch. Lumikki had been able to see even their slightest expressions.

Lumikki remembered one dark-haired actor dancing, jumping and running with particular lightness and ease. The hem of her aquamarine skirt undulated like rolling sea water. When she jumped right to the edge of the stage, though, Lumikki caught a glimpse of a knee brace under her skirt. After seeing that, Lumikki started watching the actor's expressions more carefully, noticing under the winning smile and bubbly laughter and flowing words a hint of pain. With every jump and step of the dance, over the actor's face passed a shadow that was so insignificant that it probably didn't register with anyone else. Like a fog falling over her eyes for just a split second.

Lumikki watched the actor, spellbound. She forgot to watch the rest of the play. The plot wasn't interesting any more. Lumikki stared at the changing shades of the actor's grey eyes, thinking. It was possible to take on a role that no one else could see through. You could hide pain.

The carefree dancing and laughter that filled the stage like apple blossom had become a symbol of hidden strength and power for Lumikki. She thought how she could be like this actor someday. She could choose her role and either step onto the stage or sit in the audience. Lumikki could be anyone.

Seen from the window of her train, the December afternoon seemed to darken even more quickly than normal. It was grey. Just as grey as it had been for all of October, November and the beginning of December. Today it wasn't sleeting, it was drizzling. The ground was black. The bare branches of the trees were black. Lumikki saw her reflection in the window. Her eyes looked black.

Fifteen minutes outside of Tampere Lumikki had to go to the bathroom so badly that she decided to use the restroom on the train instead of waiting until she got home. When she returned to her place, a folded sheet of paper lay on her seat.

Lumikki glanced around. No one else was in the car. Just then the train pulled up to one of the Tampere suburb stations.

Lumikki unfolded the paper with trembling hands.

My Lumikki,

I know how bad it is for you, walking past that building. I know what you went through there. And it makes me feel so furious on your behalf. If you wanted, I could make them suffer. If you wanted, I could paint the walls with their blood. I could finish what you started, your just revenge. One word from you and I would do it.

I know their names. Anna-Sofia and Vanessa. Don't think I'm not serious.

And since we're talking about names, I know other names, too. You are Lumikki, Snow White, but do you remember that there was once someone like Briar Rose, too?

Remember. You'll find her name. You haven't forgotten it, even if you might have forgotten everything else.

I'm always following you.

Your Shadow

Bile rose in Lumikki's throat. Whoever had left the note, there was no way he was on the train any more. He would have got off at that stop. The stalker had known perfectly how to time leaving his letter.

The thought that whoever wrote this had followed her to Riihimäki, kept watch to know when she was coming back and waited to see whether she would go to the bathroom nauseated Lumikki. All just to be able to leave her this anonymous message.

This wasn't a practical joke.

And no one could know the things this note said. There were things Lumikki had never told anyone. Such as the names of her tormentors.

Her phone would barely stay in Lumikki's hands they were shaking so much.

Thankfully Sampsa answered immediately.

'Can I see you today?' Lumikki asked, trying to keep her voice nonchalant.

'No.'

Lumikki swallowed.

'Why not?'

'I have band practice tonight and I've got an important project to finish, namely buying you a Christmas present,' Sampsa said with a laugh. 'So you'll have to wait until tomorrow, beautiful.'

'OK.'

Lumikki would have liked to draw out the conversation and keep hold of the safe warmth of Sampsa's voice, but she didn't dare say anything that might reveal that everything wasn't all right. So she chitchatted, telling him about her parents' holiday plans and talk of remodelling the house. The sort of small talk Lumikki never indulged in herself. But Sampsa was in a hurry, so soon Lumikki was sitting with a mute phone in her hand, staring at her reflection in the window.

In her eyes was the same defiant fear as when she was seven years old.

6

Every hit and every kick had to strike the opponent in a way that significantly reduced his fighting effectiveness. Half-hearted attacks were no benefit. They just consumed energy without helping to vanquish your enemy.

Lumikki squeezed her fingers into a fist. *Left, left, right. Left, left, right. And remember to block. Keep moving.*

How blood starts flowing from a nose when a fist contacts it. How a cheekbone breaks when a sharp kick hits it. The opponent's legs give way. He falls. He is at your mercy.

Suddenly Lumikki couldn't go on. Her feet wouldn't budge. The others continued moving to the thumping music of the Combat session, following the trainer's shouted commands, but Lumikki couldn't aim a single strike more at her imaginary foe. Of course this was just aerobics, a group exercise class spiced up with a little faux martial arts, but right now the mental images were too much.

Before her eyes Lumikki saw Anna-Sofia and Vanessa lying in the snow, beaten to within an inch of their lives. No, that hadn't really happened, but she still imagined it that way. Was her 'shadow' right? Did she still want revenge on those girls?

Lumikki had thought that coming to Combat would take her mind off the notes, but that hadn't happened. The music thundered in the gym. It stank of sweat. A few others started casting irritated glances at Lumikki because she was just standing in the middle of the gym resting her arms on her knees. *Get out of the way*, their eyes said.

As soon as her legs felt like they would carry her, Lumikki started weaving her way out of the room. She didn't even bother saying sorry when she bumped into a few of the other girls enthusiastically hitting and kicking at the air. After making it to the locker room, Lumikki headed straight for the toilet. She barely got the door locked and the lid up before the vomit gushed out of her mouth. Lumikki held the sides of the bowl, retching pieces of goat's cheese lasagne. Her whole body shook. Lumikki couldn't remember when she had last thrown up. It felt just as horrible as it ever had.

In the shower Lumikki was alone. She could still hear the Combat class outside. Coming had been a bad idea. She would have to find some other way to clear her mind. Lumikki stood under the warm water long after all the shampoo and soap had rinsed from her hair and skin. The wetness of the water was a caress. It was an embrace she could take momentary refuge in.

Lumikki tried to pinpoint the department-store speakers. She thought that if she could cast them a sufficiently searing glance, the worst Christmas ditty in the history of kitsch would end as the speakers burst into flames. Wham! released 'Last Christmas' in 1984. Wasn't it about time for it to crawl off to the pop-song graveyard and die?

Apparently department stores thought differently. Maybe someone somewhere had done a study and found that 'Last Christmas' made people buy more. There's the bitterness and pain of a broken heart, the desire for revenge and the thought that this Christmas I'll give my gifts to someone special who knows how to value them. I'll buy the most beautiful one. I'll buy the most expensive one. I'll prove my love with such a big pile of cash that no one will be able to doubt the sincerity of my feelings. But at the same time there's a sweet wistfulness, because the singer knows his broken heart still beats for the one who shattered it.

Lumikki hated this song. She hated the pre-Christmas rush. The real and imagined glitter that rested on everything, mimicking snow but really looking more like icing. The Christmas of the department stores was the one you saw in American romantic comedies, where they condensed a lifetime of sappy love and togetherness into a few winter days when everything was perfect as long as the sets and props were just so. There was a fire in the hearth and mistletoe and glittering gold and fake snow and an enormous mountain of carefully chosen presents and a full Christmas dinner and fuzzy socks and handmade chocolates and Christmas carols and the scent of cinnamon and ginger and everything so perfect you could almost gag.

That was the Christmas dream the department stores sold, and the Tampere Stockmann was no exception.

Lumikki also hated buying Christmas presents, because it felt so fake. She would prefer to give gifts when she felt like it. No matter what the date was. Buying Christmas presents was a ritual you had to perform because it was expected. Lumikki knew she couldn't not buy Sampsa a present. But she also knew the distress she would feel the moment she received some beautiful, thoughtful gift when all she had for him was something pointless and impersonal she had bought in a panic. Because Lumikki had already noticed that Sampsa was a gift giver. By some incredible instinct the boy had so far managed to give her the perfect necklace – a simple silver chain with a small black stone pendant – the world's best notebook and a pair of fingerless gloves that Lumikki always wore at home when a cold gale was blowing through the chinks in the window.

Sampsa gave his gifts lightly, without making a big deal about it. He gave gifts the way the best gifts were given – without the slightest expectation of receiving anything in return. He knew how to do it in a way that meant the other person never felt indebted or guilty. Lumikki respected that so much, but she knew she couldn't skip Christmas.

Right now it also felt necessary to be surrounded by all these bright lights and exhaustingly cheery songs. To help her shut the stalker's letters out of her mind. Lumikki didn't know what she should do about them, and because she couldn't stand uncertainty, she tried to forget about the whole thing. At least for a while. Maybe her subconscious was working on a solution.

'How about all this chintzy crap?' a voice asked behind Lumikki.

Turning, Lumikki saw Tinka and Aleksi. It was strange that they were out together on a Saturday, outside of school. Lumikki had thought they didn't really get along.

'Who would be crazy enough to actually buy something like this?' Aleksi asked. He was pointing at what had to be intended as a centrepiece – a blinking red 'I Love You' sign.

'Just imagine waking up in the middle of the night to the doorbell ringing and finding something like that sitting outside!' Tinka said, laughing. 'I'd be scared out of my mind.'

Lumikki shivered.

'I'm starting to think this might not be the best place to do my Christmas shopping,' she said, trying to keep her tone lighthearted.

'Looking for something for Sampsa?' Tinka asked quickly.

Lumikki nodded.

'Lucky boy. I'm sure you'll find the perfect thing for him.'

Lumikki thought there was a strangely melancholy shade to Tinka's smile. She didn't have the time or interest to start analysing that now, though.

'Have fun shopping!' Lumikki said and then left before the others could suggest they shop together.

Lumikki left the Stockmann Christmas department and continued down the escalator to the bottom floor. Maybe she would find something in the book department. The fact that she wasn't seeing anything she thought Sampsa would like was discouraging. Did she really know her boyfriend this poorly? Lumikki didn't want to believe that was the problem. It was just that the whole buy-buy-buy pressure always made her shut down. It made everything look stupid and tasteless.

Lumikki's hand stroked the covers of the books absent-mindedly. None of them seemed to whisper Sampsa's name.

'We have to stop meeting this way.'

The hairs on Lumikki's arms instantly stood on end. Blaze was standing next to her.

'This is twice in two days. It must be fate. Maybe now I can tempt you with a cup of coffee?'

Lumikki looked into Blaze's laughing eyes and felt herself nodding before she had time to think about her answer.

7

Two hours and four big cups of coffee later, Lumikki wondered where the past year had gone. It felt as if she and Blaze had just picked up where they had left off. Or maybe not quite there, not at the agonising final moments of their break-up. A little earlier, when the words flowed between them naturally and unforced. Now they were sitting at Lumikki's kitchen table again, just like then. Drinking coffee. Talking.

'Every day I'm happier and more whole,' Blaze said, and Lumikki could see from his direct, placid gaze that he was telling the truth.

Blaze had only told her a little about the details of the sex reassignment process, and Lumikki hadn't asked because she respected Blaze's decision to share only what he felt good sharing. This was about Blaze's body, his own physical essence.

'But I needed all the loneliness and isolation. It helped me go on, because it made me strong. I know I hurt you so much, and I want to apologise for that.'

There was an honest brightness to Blaze's words. Lumikki still couldn't reply, though, because she didn't have the words.

Instead Lumikki told him about what had happened over the previous winter and summer: the crimes she had got mixed up in, the danger and the running, how close death had been.

'I read about the thing in Prague in the newspaper. That was crazy,' Blaze said, shaking his head.

'I seem to have a habit of getting into danger,' Lumikki tried to joke, but she couldn't force a smile.

She quickly tried to cover her anxiety by taking a big gulp of coffee that was already lukewarm. That always happened to them. They barely noticed as their coffee grew cold; they had so much to say.

But Lumikki didn't tell Blaze about remembering that she used to have a sister. And of course she mentioned nothing about the harassing letters, even though she would have liked to lighten her load.

She couldn't take the risk that this 'shadow' wouldn't make good on the bloody images he painted in his messages.

Lumikki saw how her words affected Blaze. She saw the desire to protect her that sparked in his eyes. She saw how his hand moved across the table towards her own, ready to grab it.

'Oh, and I have a boyfriend,' Lumikki quickly added.

Blaze pulled his hand back and picked up his coffee cup, feigning nonchalance.

'That's great,' he said with a slanted smile.

Lumikki hurried to list all of Sampsa's wonderful qualities. Blaze listened calmly. His expression seemed to say that he didn't consider this boy a particularly important factor in Lumikki's life. His attitude slightly offended Lumikki. Did he really think he could just waltz back into Lumikki's life after pulling a stunt like disappearing for a year and that Lumikki would accept him with open arms and forget everything?

If he did, he had an infuriating amount of nerve. And he was wrong.

Blaze got up to drink a glass of water. When he returned to the table, instead of sitting down, he pressed his hands onto Lumikki's shoulders and began massaging them, as if that were perfectly natural.

'You're all knotted up,' he said.

Lumikki only managed a vague mumble in reply. She knew she should ask Blaze to stop. Theoretically a shoulder rub was just innocent touching between friends, but they weren't friends. Not again. Not only. Not yet. Maybe not ever.

Lumikki didn't ask Blaze to stop because the rubbing felt so good and her shoulders really were tighter than they had ever been before. Blaze's familiar, deft touch made them relax, and Lumikki could feel her blood flow improving as the clenching in her muscles eased. Blaze's hands were warm and their pressure was both gentle and purposeful. He didn't try to force her muscles into submission. First he massaged lightly, then gradually pressed harder and deeper. He stopped at the tighter spots and took the time to warm them under his fingers.

Florence + the Machine played in the background, singing about bruised bodies burning with passionate fire. Lumikki regretted her choice of music. But not really. She had known what she was doing when she put Florence on. She had known what mood it would create.

Blaze's touch made Lumikki slip into a sweet, almost dreamlike state. For a moment she could forget everything else. The fear. The anxiety. She didn't need to think anything. The languid relaxation and warmth spread from her shoulders down.

Lumikki didn't know how long had passed when she realised the massaging had changed. Now it was more caressing. Blaze gently stroked her neck, and every brush of his hand made shivers run down Lumikki's spine and beyond. Gradually the relaxation melted away, replaced by a burning fire inside. Blaze's hands brushed the sides of her neck and her earlobes, and then returned to the nape of her neck. Warm breath against Lumikki's skin.

The two of them against each other, chest to chest, breath heavy, lips touching.

The two of them in the shower, bare, slick skin, wet, the hard tile wall behind her back, sounds echoing in the small room.

The two of them on Lumikki's bed, the tangled sheets, the panting, the teeth on her shoulder, the cries they couldn't hold back.

The two of them in their own forest, surrounded by the scent of pine, hidden, concealed in the shadows, clinging to each other, lost in each other, somewhere far away, far above in the branches, the twinkling light of the stars.

Lumikki snapped out of her daydream. Quickly she shrugged Blaze's hands from her shoulders, stood up and stepped away from him.

'You need to go now.'

Lumikki stared past Blaze with determination. She couldn't take the risk of looking him in the eye. Then maybe she wouldn't have the strength to drive him away.

Blaze didn't ask any questions. Calmly he went to the hallway, picked up his coat and wrapped up in silence for the cold outside. But at the door he turned and smiled.

'I'll see you again soon, my princess. You know it as well as I do. We can't stay away from each other for long.'

Then he left without waiting for Lumikki's reply.

Lumikki stood staring at the door. She knew that Blaze was right.

I've seen so often how people can be truly, senselessly cruel to each other. Especially in school. Children and teenagers find each other's vulnerabilities and strike at them without mercy. They are animals. School is a hunting ground and a battlefield. Only the strong survive.

That is really why I dream about carrying out my threats. Everyone watching the play. Everyone quiet in their seats.

Then the stage fills with shouts and blood and bodies. Panic. The doors locked. Then it's the audience's turn. One at a time. No one would escape. I would paint the whole theatre red.

Life's but a walking shadow, a poor player
That struts and frets his hour upon the stage
And then is heard no more: it is a tale
Told by an idiot, full of sound and fury,
Signifying nothing.

They would learn that even the strongest, the most brutal, the most cunning are not invincible. They would learn it the hard way.
By the laws of life and death.

SUNDAY, 10 DECEMBER

8

Lumikki was jealous. She realised she had never felt this so strongly before in her life. She had wanted to be someone else before. Someone who wouldn't need to hide the bruises at home and suck blood from her lower lip and claim that she had just tripped and fallen. But that had been more of a hopeless desire to escape her own life than actual jealousy.

Sampsa's father was just carrying in a big pile of pancakes and setting them on the table.

'These aren't going to win any prizes,' he said.

'Well, what do you expect when the whole time you were cooking them you had one eye on that iPad game of yours?' Sampsa's mother pointed out and patted her husband's arm.

Sampsa's little sister, Saara, was rocking in her chair.

'I'm going to eat at least six pancakes!' she announced.

'How does a penguin make pancakes?' Sampsa asked.

'Um, how?' his sister replied.

'With its flippers!'

'What? Oh . . .' Saara said as the punchline dawned on her, and she began laughing infectiously.

'OK, here's another one,' he said. 'What dinosaur loves pancakes the most?'

'What?' Saara asked.

'Tri-syrup-tops!'

At which point Saara nearly fell on the floor giggling.

'I'm here all week, folks,' Sampsa said, looking smug.

'I blame their sense of humour on you,' Sampsa's mother said to his father.

Sampsa's dad shrugged, grinning proudly.

Lumikki watched the exchange in bewilderment.

She wasn't used to being in a family like this where people joked and laughed all the time. Sampsa's family also seemed to talk nonstop. Words launched back and forth between them like balls being tossed around, some of them landing on the floor without anyone paying any attention. The communication might seem like chaos, but apparently it wasn't. Everyone more or less kept up. Even Saara, who was only four.

A certain amount of tender chaos characterised Sampsa's house in other ways, too. Even the most generous person could never have called it tidy. There was stuff all over the place – toys strewn across the floor, clothes draped over chairs, piles of magazines and books, half-opened boxes and parcels that might be either coming or going. Lumikki's parents' house could never have looked like that.

Lumikki envied Sampsa's family so much it made her heart ache. Everything showed that their life was here and now. They took care of each other and enjoyed each other's company. They had fun. They were natural and unforced, without anything contrived or fake or pretend about them, even when a stranger like Lumikki was visiting. They had accepted her like a long-lost relative expected to participate in everything that was going on. Lumikki had never felt so welcomed anywhere as when she had stepped over the threshold of Sampsa's parents' home. Her own father's Swedish-Finnish extended family had always felt distant to Lumikki, even though they had their own happy songs and liked to talk. Every time she was with them, Lumikki felt like the black sheep, whom everyone wished was different, happier and more sociable. Sampsa's family was like Sampsa himself: without any demands or expectations.

Out of the corner of her eye, Lumikki watched Sampsa, relaxed and smiling broadly as he piled pancakes onto his little sister's plate. Lumikki knew she could never look like that with her own family.

Everything was so good in Sampsa's life. His happiness was self-evident and completely deserved. He was a person who had room to be friendly and warm to others. In his world there weren't any silent secrets or threatening letters or the fear of death. In his world a girlfriend wasn't supposed to let her ex-boyfriend massage her neck knowing full well the forbidden desire his touch would arouse.

Lumikki watched the bustle of Sampsa's family and suddenly felt chillingly alone. Her fear, her dark places, her anger that ran as red as blood, the black shadows of her forest, her murky waters and deep undercurrents – they would never be part of these people's lives. These happy, sunny, joking, playful, loud, almost irritatingly voluble and perfectly lovely people's lives.

'Now my hands are sticky!' Saara said, holding up red palms.

In the end she had only managed to eat three pancakes.

'Well, you did eat half a gallon of strawberry jam on your pancakes. And you ate with your hands.'

Sampsa leaned over to wipe his sister's hands with a napkin. Sticky strawberry jam. Red. Sticky. Warm. Blood.

Images flashed through Lumikki's head so fast she couldn't catch hold of them. In her mind she saw jam dripping onto the floor. She saw a pool of blood that grew and grew. She shook her head a little. Where were these images coming from?

'Can I go play now?' Saara asked impatiently.

'Yes,' her mother replied.

'Lumikki is going to come play princesses with me,' Saara declared, grabbing Lumikki's hand with her own, still slightly sticky, one.

Lumikki flinched at the touch. A bloody hand. A hand that didn't move even though she nudged it. A slowly cooling hand.

'Lumikki might still want to eat. Ask nicely,' Sampsa's father said.

'Yes, I can come,' Lumikki said quickly.

She wanted to get her mind away from the strange images that kept flashing and disappearing before her eyes like lightning strikes.

Saara put a frilly lace hat on Lumikki's head before pulling a pink dress over her own clothes and waving her magic wand.

'This is a magic wand and a sword at the same time,' she explained proudly, showing off the sparkling stick.

'That's handy. If monsters come you can cast a spell on them and make them nice, or fight them off,' Lumikki said.

The lace hat itched on her head, but she let it be. She could stand a little discomfort during the game.

'Monsters are my friends. But if the evil Prince comes, I'll chop off his head. And then I'll turn him into a cute little frog.'

Lumikki smiled. Apparently this family had turned the traditional fairy-tale roles on their heads several times over. Saara started dancing wildly in her pink princess dress. Little Briar Rose.

The last letter flashed back into Lumikki's mind. She tried to push it into the background, but it wouldn't go. Its words barged back to the forefront, hitting her like waves rolling against the shore one after another. Ever higher, breaking white.

Briar Rose. Rose.

Lumikki had to sit on the floor because her legs were about to give way. This wasn't a dream or a fumbling fantasy. This was real. This was a memory.

Rose. Rosa.

Her sister's name had been Rosa.

MONDAY, 11 DECEMBER

9

Lumikki pressed herself flat against the cold stone wall of the tower room. She stayed perfectly silent and still. First she became only a shadow, then part of the stone wall as she melted into it. Lumikki became hard. Her legs and arms froze. Her heart became a rock. Her breath slowed to nothing. She did not exist.

Lumikki knew that the door of the tower room would open, that she would only have a few seconds. She would have to strike instantly. In her hand she squeezed the silver comb, stroking its sharp teeth with a finger. If she pressed her fingertip against a tooth, it would sink into her skin and make great drops of blood well up. The winding, beautiful ornamental embossing of the comb felt comforting and safe against her hand. It formed an image of intertwining roses.

Briar Rose. Who pricked her finger on a spinning wheel and slept for a century. Rosa, who slept the eternal sleep. Lumikki's sister. No, she couldn't think about that now.

She had to concentrate on when the door would open. All her senses and thoughts had to be harnessed for this.

Lumikki heard footsteps approaching. She could tell from their rhythm that the person coming was the one she was waiting for. She hated him so much that her rage nearly blinded her with a jagged haze of red across her vision. Her captor, her oppressor, who had killed the only person Lumikki could imagine loving. Lumikki hated him so much she was ready to kill.

The steps paused at the door. The key turned excruciatingly slowly in the lock. Lumikki squeezed the comb in her hand. As the Prince walked in, the opening door concealed Lumikki. The Prince looked around at the empty tower room, confused. Lumikki kicked the door shut and attacked. With a single, violent thrust, she plunged the sharp teeth of the comb into the Prince's neck. The Prince fell, holding his throat.

Blood. Red and warm. The elixir of life, pulsing with every heartbeat out of the Prince, every leaking drop bringing him closer to death.

'Help,' the Prince beseeched Lumikki as he died.

'Never.'

Lumikki stood in the Prince's blood and watched as the life began to disappear from his face. She didn't hurry. She enjoyed the moment. 'Die, my tormentor. You wanted to lull me into an eternal sleep and close me back up in a glass coffin. You wanted to look at me as if I were nothing more than a beautiful, silent decoration. Not a living person with thoughts and feelings and desires. Difficult to control. My own independent being, who doesn't always do exactly what you want.'

'Good, good. Very good, Lumikki. Keep that.'

Excitedly Tinka jumped onto the stage and put her hand on Lumikki's arm. Lumikki recoiled. She realised how hard she was breathing. Her hands were shaking and she was almost surprised when they weren't bloody. She had felt the warm, sticky blood on them. Sticky like strawberry jam. Once again Lumikki had been somewhere else, so deep in her role that everything had actually been happening to her.

'Is that really believable, that she just stands there watching me die? Shouldn't she run away or something?' Aleksi asked, rubbing his neck.

'This is an important climax. Snow White's revenge. Of course she has to stop and watch for a few seconds. The audience has to stop. And this isn't supposed to be realistic.'

Tinka's voice was irritated again, as it so often was when she spoke to Aleksi.

'OK, OK. You're the director. Your vision,' Aleksi replied.

Then he leaned over to Lumikki.

'Could you go a little easier with the comb next time? You scratched me pretty badly with it.'

Aleksi showed the red marks on his neck.

'Yeah, sorry.'

What Lumikki couldn't say was how surprised she was that Aleksi's neck wasn't spurting real blood. She couldn't remember a moment when she could have stopped her attack.

'That's a wrap for tonight,' Tinka said and clapped her hands.

Everybody started collecting their things. Sampsa came over to Lumikki and wrapped his arm around her.

'Tonight I'm going to come over to your place for the night and we can play Snow White and the Huntsman,' he whispered into Lumikki's ear.

'The Huntsman died,' Lumikki said with a snort. 'I'm not sure I'm really into the necrophilia thing.'

'I might rise from the dead with the right encouragement.'

Watching their whispering, Tinka's eyes narrowed ever so slightly. 'Let's go before we have to get those two a room.'

Aleksi laughed. Lumikki couldn't quite put a finger on Tinka's tone of voice. Maybe there was a little jealousy in it, but was there something else? Something darker? A hard edge under the sarcasm?

In the mirrored foyer a strange sight awaited them.

Red rose petals had been scattered all over the floor.

'OK, who's the funny man?' Tinka asked the others.

Everyone just looked at each other and shrugged.

'Nobody else should be here but us,' Sampsa pointed out.

'Hello? Anybody here?' Tinka yelled loudly.

Here, here, here, echoed down the empty hallways. No one answered.

'Strange,' Aleksi said.

Lumikki looked at the petals. Their heady, sickly scent filled her nostrils. She knew the roses were meant for her. Her stalker wanted to remind her of Briar Rose. Apparently he didn't know that Lumikki had already remembered her sister's name. That brought her some degree of satisfaction. Lumikki knew that in at least one area she was ahead of her stalker.

Once upon a time there was a key that fitted a small chest. Two little girls often played with the chest. It was their treasure chest, where they hid jewellery and rocks and bird feathers and perfect pinecones and beautiful autumn leaves and corks and marbles and all the secrets they shared. They were princesses, and when they grew up they would use the riches in the chest to travel around the world.

Then came the day when the chest was emptied. All of the girls' wonderful treasures disappeared. The chest was filled with other kinds of treasures and secrets. But no one could use them to travel around the world. And besides, one of the girls would never travel anywhere ever again.

Once upon a time there was a key that had waited long and patiently.

Once upon a time there was a key that wanted to open the chest again and reveal its secrets.

Once upon a time there was a key that was moved from its old hiding place to wait in a new hiding place, in a cold crevice of rock.

TUESDAY, 12 DECEMBER,
EARLY MORNING

10

Lumikki woke up hot and anxious. She glanced at her phone. It was 3:20 in the morning. A time when she should have been happily sleeping the deepest sleep possible. Sampsa's arm was wrapped around her, the boy radiating warmth. Usually that felt good, but right now it was too much heat. Wriggling out from under his arm, she climbed out of bed. Sampsa mumbled in his sleep but then rolled over and continued his quiet snoring. Happily sleeping away in perfect safety. Lumikki looked at the back of Sampsa's head and his mussed hair, slowly letting herself fill with the tenderness she felt for him.

Sweet, sweet Sampsa. Sleeping like an innocent child. Strangely innocent even when awake. Fearless because he'd never really had to fear. Knowing his own worth because no one had ever called it into question or trampled it into the ground.

Lumikki closed the door behind her as she went into the kitchen. She turned on the light and tried to decide whether to make coffee. Then she definitely wouldn't be able to get back to sleep, but right now she really needed that strong smell and familiar taste. The bite of that first sip, which soon turned into a sensuous feeling of relaxation and refreshment. Sharpening her senses.

She was just about to grab the espresso pot when she noticed her phone display light up. A text message. Who on earth would be texting her at this hour of the morning?

My Lumikki, you're awake. I can see the light burning in your window. Don't even think about waking up your slumbering boyfriend. This is just between the two of us, like all important things.

Lumikki's mouth went dry. It was hard to swallow. Breathing felt difficult. The text message had been sent through an anonymous server, so the phone only displayed the provider's number, not the sender's. Her stalker was leaving nothing to chance – he hadn't left any traces of himself, even by accident.

Escape. Hide. Lights off.

That was Lumikki's first reaction, but she knew all of that was pointless. She had already been seen. She couldn't hide. So with as steady a step as she could manage, she walked to the window and looked out into the darkness. She forbade her hands from shaking and pressed them against the glass, shading a small peephole for herself out into the outside world. There was no one in the park. The shadows of the trees didn't move. But there were too many dark places where her stalker could be hidden to count. Or he could be in the building opposite. He could be standing almost anywhere. He could see Lumikki. Lumikki couldn't see him.

Another text.

Come out. I want to show you something.

Never. Lumikki nearly threw her phone against the wall. Did this person think she lacked any sense of self-preservation? That she was just going to walk out into the night because some lunatic was sending her messages? Lumikki knew she was reckless sometimes, but she wasn't *that* crazy.

Lumikki sat down at the table and looked at her phone. She could turn it off. Her stalker could send her messages all night if he wanted, but she wasn't going to read any of them.

Just then a third text came through.

I can see you aren't going to come out. Too bad. In that case I'll have to do something else tonight. I have Anna-Sofia's address here. I think I'll pay her a visit. Do you have anything you'd like me to say to her? If you do, now's the time. In the morning she won't be able to hear it any more. Or anything else.

Lumikki stood up so fast the chair clattered to the floor. The person sending these messages had to be bluffing. What a bullshit threat. He wasn't going to kill Anna-Sofia. He couldn't. He was just trying to see how far he could push Lumikki.

But what if he was serious . . .?

Or have you changed your mind? You have two choices, Lumikki. Either you come outside now or Anna-Sofia dies

before sunrise. Maybe you want her to die. If you do, I'm happy to oblige. Anything for you, my love.

Lumikki knew she couldn't take the risk. She didn't know who she was dealing with, but she knew that this stalker knew things about her he shouldn't be able to know. And he really could be prepared to do anything.

Clothes on. Coat on. Boots on. One last careful peek in to make sure Sampsa was sleeping. Still the same quiet, peaceful snoring. Lumikki quickly scribbled a note saying she couldn't sleep and had gone out for a walk. She sincerely hoped Sampsa wouldn't wake up before she got back. If she got back.

No, Lumikki didn't give in to fear, even though it washed over her in a choking deluge.

Outside it was drizzling. Before letting the door swing shut, Lumikki squeezed the door handle so hard her hand started to hurt. She looked around, but didn't see anyone. What kind of game was this? She had come outside. She was following instructions.

Another text message.

Good girl. But the night is cold. I want to take you somewhere warm. I know you're a fast runner. You have exactly fifteen minutes to run to Milavida Palace. If you don't make it in time, I'll change my plans after all and go kill Anna-Sofia. Your time starts now.

Lumikki had already set off running as she read the final words of the message. The wet, slick park path seemed to slip away under her combat boots. Why hadn't she thought to put on running shoes? She should have learned by now that she always ended up running at some point. That was what her life had turned into since last February.

In her mind, Lumikki quickly calculated the fastest route. To the end of the park, across the railroad tracks and then straight to the river. Grey-brown muck squelched under her boots. The cold drizzle penetrated her coat and hat, and reduced visibility. The street lamps shone wanly. Everywhere their light didn't reach was as black as pitch.

As she ran and glanced at the time, Lumikki wondered if there was any sense to this. Why was she doing it? Why did she really care whether her stalker carried out his threat? Lumikki hadn't seen Anna-Sofia in more than two years and hadn't had anything to do with her otherwise. It shouldn't have mattered to Lumikki in the slightest what happened to her former school bully.

When Lumikki crossed the tracks and turned north towards the river, she realised this was the only thing she could do, because a part of her really did want Anna-Sofia to die. Lumikki had fantasised about it so many times, sometimes even dreaming it would happen. Even after she got away from her tormentors and moved to Tampere. A small part of Lumikki thirsted for revenge and the feeling that evil had received its reward. Because of Anna-Sofia and Vanessa, she had spent years wishing she could be dead instead of having to endure their torture.

Justified revenge.

If Lumikki had just stayed at home and gone back to sleep and Anna-Sofia had really died, she would have felt responsible. She would have felt guilty, because a part of her wanted it.

Still five minutes left. Lumikki pounded along the street. She was just coming to the footbridge that led over the river to the park where the palace was. The bridge was wet. The cold, damp air was no good for her lungs. But she would make it. She had to make it.

This park wasn't one of Lumikki's favourite places. It was beautiful enough, with a long history – it had been built almost on bare rock back in the early 1800s. In the summer it was intoxicatingly green and had amazing views out over the lake. There were all kinds of different rock-dwelling plants, fences built from river stones, and the park even had Finland's biggest poplar tree. Under different circumstances, Lumikki would have thought it the best park in Tampere.

But Blaze had dumped her here. That was why Lumikki could never come here without experiencing a confused mixture of sadness and anxiety. Now the park was as black and silent as the grave. A nightmare park.

The palace rose white and woefully rundown in the centre of the park, on the highest spot, in stately solitude. Lumikki's lungs hurt as she expended the last of her strength on the uphill stretch.

Milavida. That was the original, melodious name of the place. Milavida's history was tragic. The owner of the Finlayson textile factory, Wilhelm von Nottbeck's son Peter von Nottbeck, had built it as a replacement for the family's previous house, a villa next to the rocky hill where the palace now stood. However, the Nottbeck family never lived in their new house, which was completed in 1898, because Peter's wife, Olga, died giving birth to twins, and Peter died six months later after an appendix operation in a Paris hospital. The palace was sold to the City of Tampere in 1905. In the black December night, Milavida looked like the ethereal ghost of a building. A palace of spectres. Perhaps the Nottbecks had moved in after all following their deaths.

Lumikki looked at her phone. She had made it in time. She felt like screaming for her stalker to come out and show himself at last. Just then a new text message arrived.

One minute early. You were faster than I expected. You've earned your reward. In the foundations of the palace, on the left-hand side with your back to the lake, is a small hole. There's something for you there.

First a game of Tag and now Hide and Seek. The stalker must be getting some sick pleasure from all this. Lumikki went to the left side of the building and started feeling along the cold stone foundations with her fingers. Nothing. No hole. She was getting tired of this. Then, just as she was about to give up and her fingers were losing all feeling, she found a crack almost at ground level. She pushed her fingers in and caught hold of something metal. Lumikki pulled it out.

In her hand lay a small brass key.

Congratulations. This is the key to the great secret of your life. I'm sure once you remember enough you'll also remember what the key is for. But now it's time for you

73

to go and make sure your prince is sleeping safely. You wouldn't want anything bad to happen to him. Even if he isn't your one true love.

Lumikki would never have thought she could run back even faster. Fear gave her wings. If this lunatic did anything to Sampsa . . .

At home everything was as it should have been. Sampsa was asleep in bed. Lumikki took off her clothes, crumpled up the note she'd written earlier and threw it in the bin, and snuck back into bed. In his sleep, Sampsa turned over and hugged her. His fringe was moist. Had he had a nightmare and been sweating?

Suddenly Lumikki was so tired that her eyes drooped shut. She fell into a sleep free of nightmares or dreams about the mysterious key waiting in her coat pocket. The key with the heart.

People are so trusting. If you're assertive and credible enough, they swallow every word you say and love how true they taste. That's why it was ultimately so easy to get the key. People trust me and end up saying things they wouldn't otherwise. All I had to do was create a relaxed, confidential mood and even he talked. And you should never forget that alcohol helps people open up, too. The key was hidden where he guessed.

'Isn't it sick that they still keep it in the bookshelf behind a copy of Tittytumpkin's Fairy Tree?' That's what he said when I got him drunk. I agreed, although I think there are much sicker things in this world. Who am I to judge other people's decisions? We all want to keep our secrets in our own way.

I wanted to give it to you so you would remember. I could just tell you everything I know, but that would be boring. I would rather you found it out for yourself. Then it will mean more. Then your own, real memories will come back.

You may not be able to think of it this way yet, but I am giving you gifts. One at a time. And these are the biggest gifts anyone has ever given you.

I am giving you your past.

I am giving you your secret.

I am giving you who you really are.

I am giving you yourself. Finally.

And then you will be prepared to accept my final gift, my eternal love, because you understand that I am the only person who can love you this much. Then you will learn to love me, too. We are the same. We are one.

TUESDAY, 12 DECEMBER

11

The black water dragged Lumikki ever further down. She couldn't have reached the surface even if she tried. But she didn't want to try. Under the water was a forest. Different from any forest on land. The trunks and branches of the trees were in constant, fluid motion. They were flexible. They were soft water plants.

Lumikki sank deeper and deeper. Now she could see something shining on the bottom of the lake. It was a small chest. It looked familiar. Lumikki realised that the brass key she had been given would fit the lock on the chest. They belonged together.

Lumikki tried to get to the chest, but suddenly her feet became stuck in the black muck of the lakebed. She couldn't move. She couldn't breathe. Her oxygen was running out. Lumikki knew that her lungs would soon fill with water and she would die.

'Fear.'

Hearing this word stated emphatically snapped Lumikki awake. She had just nodded off. It took her a few seconds to remember that she was in psychology class and that the teacher's voice had woken her up. Running to Milavida Palace the night before felt like a distant nightmare, but two concrete pieces of evidence remained. Insane exhaustion and the small brass key that was in Lumikki's jeans pocket, tempting her to finger it over and over again.

The chest. She remembered the chest. But where had she seen it . . .?

'Fear is one of the primary drivers of human behaviour,' the teacher, Henrik Virta, continued. 'Sometimes I wonder if we should even talk about courage. Perhaps there's no such thing as courage. Only fear.'

'How do you justify that?' Tinka asked without raising her hand.

'We often hear that courage is the conquering of fear. As I see it, fear itself is what drives us to act and can make us do things we wouldn't be able to otherwise. So fear looks like courage.'

Henrik's voice was deep and pleasant. He had always been one of Lumikki's favourite teachers, specifically because he knew how to say things in a way that made you think but wasn't too provocative.

'But doesn't fear make you run and courage makes you stay and fight?' Aleksi asked.

'You can think of it that way. But you can also argue that fear gives us instructions about how it's best to act in any given situation. The fear of death is one of the strongest. And sometimes it makes us run away, but other times it motivates us to fight,' Henrik said.

Lumikki was still tired and would have liked to just lay her head on her arms on her desk and sleep, sleep, sleep. Sitting next to her, Sampsa stroked Lumikki's arm.

'Go home after class and take a nap. You look like the walking dead,' he whispered.

'Thanks,' Lumikki snorted.

In the morning Sampsa had remarked on how exhausted Lumikki looked. Lumikki had just said that she hadn't been able to sleep very well. What else could she have said? Her stalker was very clear that she wasn't allowed to breathe a word about him or his messages to anyone. Sampsa thought Lumikki should have just stayed home from school, but she felt like she couldn't stand being alone today. Rest sounded good now, though. It sounded imperative.

After class had ended, Henrik asked Lumikki to stay behind for a few minutes. Sampsa had to hurry to his next class, so he just raised his hand to his ear signalling that he would call her later. Lumikki nodded in reply.

'I just wanted to check and make sure you're planning to take the psychology college entrance exam in the spring,' Henrik said.

'I guess,' Lumikki replied.

'I wouldn't ask, but you're definitely the most talented student I've had in years. We aren't supposed to say things like that, but I wanted you to know.'

Henrik patted Lumikki lightly on the shoulder.

'OK. Thanks,' Lumikki said, off balance.

She was relieved when Henrik turned back to his papers, indicating that their conversation was over. Lumikki needed sleep so badly it was painful.

* * *

The doorbell rang just as Lumikki was dreaming about kissing Blaze. In her dream, she felt the brass key slip from her mouth into his.

Lumikki got out of bed still wrapped in the dream. She peered through the peephole.

Blaze. Of course. Lumikki wasn't even surprised.

She opened the door even though she had promised herself she wasn't going to let Blaze in any more. The kiss from the dream still tingled on her lips, though. At first Blaze didn't say anything. Taking off his orange gloves, he lightly stroked Lumikki's cheek with cool fingers.

'I had to come,' he said. 'Ever since our last meeting I've had this feeling you were afraid of something. I had to come and make sure you were all right. You know I would protect you from any of the evils in this world.'

These words struck Lumikki like burning arrows. Something inside her cracked and crumbled.

Because someone could see her so clearly. Could sense the emotions she tried so hard to hide.

Lumikki grabbed Blaze by the neck and pulled him into her. She gazed into his eyes as long as she could. Plunging into the ice water. Jumping into the blue of the sky. Stepping into the hottest, blue-white incandescent place in the fire. Then she kissed Blaze and let her lips and mouth and tongue communicate all the longing and misery and desire and passion that had been tearing her apart since they broke up.

As soon as the kiss began, Lumikki knew.

This was their forest. This was their lake. This was their ink-black, clear sky full of points of light.

All these things surrounded them simultaneously: nothing had disappeared. The light finding its tiny paths through the leaves of the trees, the calming dark, the rustling, the scratching, the cooing, the soughing of the wind, the lapping, the gently rocking waves, the cool currents and warm pockets of water, the feeling of weightlessness, the giddiness, the immensity, time and eternity, the air that flowed freely into their lungs, the pulse of the universe, their shared heart.

Lumikki couldn't remember when she had last felt something as hard and unpleasant as breaking away from that kiss. But she had to.

How could something that felt so right be so wrong?

'We can't see each other. At least for a while. I'm with Sampsa now,' Lumikki managed to say.

She had forced herself to take a step backwards. The distance between her and Blaze felt painfully long. They should have been right up against each other. But they couldn't.

'Do you love him?' Blaze asked.

He asked it in such a serious tone that he deserved an honest answer from Lumikki.

'I'm not sure I know what love is,' she said.

'Why are you with him then? Why are you pushing me away? Is it because he's a real boy?'

Exhaustion washed over Lumikki.

'Of course not. Don't even joke about that.'

'If I'm not good enough for you, just say so. If I'm too incomplete, too imperfect.'

Lumikki heard the hurt and sadness in Blaze's voice, but she couldn't comfort him. Not now.

'This isn't going to go this way,' was all she said.

How could she explain to Blaze that everything felt so perfect when she was with him? It felt like nothing was missing. But she was with Sampsa now, and Sampsa was nice and sweet and dependable. Sampsa had never broken her heart.

Lumikki knew that if she took one more step into the forest, if she swam two more strokes into the lake, if she let the starry sky descend and fill her soul, she would never get out. She would never want to get out. And she didn't believe she could stand having that all taken away from her again. Blaze had done it once. Blaze had gone and taken the forest and the lake and the stars away. Lumikki couldn't trust that Blaze wouldn't do it again. Lumikki didn't dare allow herself to be hurt again.

'You can't do this to me,' Blaze said. 'I was only able to make it through all of this because of you. So we could be together again. And now you're turning your back on me.'

You turned your back on me, Lumikki thought. *But this isn't revenge. I'm not doing this to you. You're doing this to yourself. I'm punishing myself more than you, denying myself happiness because I'm too afraid. I just can't step into the dark and fall again. I would die. I would go crazy.*

But all she said was, 'You went through all of that for yourself. As it should be. No one else can make you happy and complete but you.'

Lumikki saw Blaze's eyes well up. Their surface quivered, but he just managed to hold back enough to keep the tears from rolling down his cheeks. This suppressed pain hurt Lumikki more than if Blaze had started to cry. She had to strain not to wrap her arms around Blaze and hug him for a long time, oh so long.

'You are a cold creature, Lumikki. I thought I knew you.'

Lumikki did not reply. She didn't have the words. If Blaze chose to be bitter and hate her, that might make things easier for him. It would be easier for him to break free of her.

When the door slammed shut behind Blaze, Lumikki's legs gave way. Collapsing on the hall floor, she felt the blackness creep over her from the shadows in the corners. It penetrated her ears and nostrils, wriggling down her throat into her lungs and stomach, filling them. Breathing was hard. She was running out of air.

Finally Lumikki stood up and walked to the kitchen. She needed some strong coffee now. Blacker than the blackness that had made its home inside her. As Lumikki measured the coffee into the pot, she heard the letterbox bang.

A familiar fear sank its carnivorous teeth into her neck.

Probably just junk mail, Lumikki thought.

But instead, a white sheet of paper folded over once sat on the floor in the hallway. Lumikki shoved open the door and rushed into the stairwell. No one. Not even running steps on the stairs. The lift was still. Lumikki hesitated for a moment but then went back inside. She wasn't going to go chasing a shadow. The worst thing that could happen might be catching him.

Lumikki didn't want to open the letter, but she couldn't not open it. All it said was:

I love you more than anyone else. Always.

Your touch makes me feel alive. Living feels worth it then.

I've dreamed of you for so long. I've read all the newspaper stories about you. The ones they wrote last summer when you saved those people from the burning building. When I was reading them, I thought that you were a hero but that the reporters didn't know you. They wrote about you as if you were just a clever or brave girl. They didn't see the fierceness in your eyes.

I know you're like me. Part of you wanted to watch as the fire consumed that building and those people. You have the element of destruction inside you. You hide it because our society doesn't approve, but we children of destruction and ruin recognise our own kind.

I have dreamed about everything I would do to you if you would give yourself completely to me. All the ways I would touch you. Ways you've never even dreamed of. I know I could make you completely lose control. You would beg me to stop. You would beg me to go on.

Your touch would arouse the beast in me.

But we are both beasts of prey, my Lumikki. We are the ones they try to kill in the fairy tales. We do not die. We always exist in the dark places, behind trees, underground, in deep waters.

The day will come when you are completely mine. That day is coming faster than you know.

WEDNESDAY, 13 DECEMBER

12

Lumikki burrowed deeper under the covers. She never wanted to leave this warm nest where she could momentarily be far away from the evil world.

The sleet could lash the windows. The cold could try to creep through the chinks in the window frames. Under this blanket she had a false security.

Björk was playing in Lumikki's head despite the apartment's silence, singing about playing dead to make the hurting stop. Lumikki imagined an arm around her, warm breath on her neck, a body pressed against her back. She felt it. She felt the hand caressing her shoulder. She felt skin against her skin. She felt the lips that touched her lips and whose kiss made her own mouth open, made her open.

Lumikki felt Blaze. As strongly as if he were really next to her. Lumikki finally understood that this was just the way it was. Blaze lived inside of her, even if they were apart. Even if they would never see each other again. Blaze was the one whose hand Lumikki would feel squeezing hers when she was afraid walking in the dark at night. Blaze was the one whose body heat would radiate into Lumikki when she was sitting in an armchair reading a book. Blaze was the one whose gentle touch would caress her to sleep when she was lying alone. Not Sampsa.

Lumikki felt Sampsa when he was there. When Sampsa was against her. When Sampsa's arms were around her waist and his lips were nuzzling her neck. Then Lumikki didn't feel anything else or think of anyone else. They were just present for each other. At least that was what she told herself. But when Sampsa was gone, he was gone. Lumikki didn't feel him next to her like she felt Blaze.

Was that wrong?

Could you live like that?

Lumikki couldn't help her feelings. She couldn't deny them or wish them out of existence. She wasn't going to be able to erase the intimacy she felt with Blaze just by force of will, given that more than a year of separation hadn't done it. The feeling wasn't wrong.

But she could decide what her actions would be. She could decide what decisions she would make. She had chosen Sampsa. He signified safety; Blaze signified pain. That was just how it was.

Lumikki threw off her blanket and immediately felt the chill. The hard, cold floor brought her body back to reality one toe at a time. She had to venture into the outside world, to school and the hard, piercing gaze of the bright electric lights, which would scare her nightmares away and wipe her skin clean of the memory of Blaze's touch.

* * *

Celestial brilliance, triumphal decree.
Proclaiming the Advent for all to see.

The starry sky burns clear and bright,
Set the candles alight, the candles alight.

The school stairs had been turned into a candle-lined corridor. All the other lights had been shut off. The living dance of the flickering candle flames momentarily made the school look like a fairy-tale castle or nineteenth-century manor house. Lumikki hadn't remembered that this morning would start with the St Lucia procession. Lately the tradition had begun spreading from Swedish-speaking circles to Finnish ones as well.

Lumikki always felt conflicted about St Lucia's Day. There was something warm and safe about it that felt good deep down inside, but there were also unpleasant memories. One year, just before she started school, Lumikki had wanted to play Lucia at home. Her daycare in Riihimäki hadn't adopted the Lucia tradition yet. Her mother had been delighted at the idea and promised to bake Lucia buns and make a white robe and crown of candles for Lumikki to wear. But her father had just looked at Lumikki long and hard, his face overshadowed by a greyness that drained all expression away.

'This family is not going to celebrate a woman who tore her own eyes out to stop a man from molesting her because of her beauty. Who was killed by a dagger stuck in her throat after burning her to death didn't work.'

Lumikki still remembered her father's words. She remembered how her excitement had died. As if she had been forced to swallow icicles whole. Her mother had been furious with her father for saying anything so gruesome to a child. But for Lumikki, it wasn't her father's words that hurt. The worst thing

93

had been the way he looked right through her, as if neither she nor her eagerness nor her joy even existed in his eyes.

Lumikki had never suggested celebrating St Lucia's Day again.

Now she watched as a group of high-school girls descended the stairs in long white dresses, green paper garlands on their heads, tea lights in their hands. Tinka walked at their head. Her long red hair was an angelic cloud of curls. As she passed Lumikki she smiled sweetly and squinted a bit.

When the procession moved on into the mirrored foyer and the girls' singing began to fade, Lumikki found the words repeating in her mind in Swedish.

Stjärnor som leda oss, vägen att finna,
bli dina klara bloss, fagra prästinna.
Drömmar med vingesus, under oss sia,
tänd dina vita ljus, Sankta Lucia.

Finnish had always been Lumikki's stronger language. She used her Swedish much less frequently. Mostly just with her dad and his relatives. Nevertheless, for her, Swedish was the language of poetry, a language of song that strummed chords of emotion within her that lacked any names.

Drömmar med vingesus.

Vingesus. How could so much beauty fit in one single word? Wings. The rustling of wings. Or soughing, like the soughing of the wind. Roaring like rapids or the raging of fire. Lumikki heard the word in her ears in melodic tones, sung by the clear voice of a child. The voice was familiar, but it wasn't her own.

Suddenly, she saw wooden steps before her, with a little girl running down them singing 'Sankta Lucia' in Swedish. Rosa. This had to be her lost sister Rosa. She remembered how beautiful Rosa had looked to her, somehow heavenly, and how she had thought that the next year she wanted to be singing with Rosa. Why didn't she have any memory of the following year? Hadn't the next year come?

In her memory, Rosa smiled tenderly at Lumikki. As only an older sister could smile.

The Prince laced Lumikki's corset tighter.

Just a little more and you will be an obedient wife.

Just a little more and you will learn to behave with more virtue and restraint. You aren't living in the woods any more. You are a queen. You must walk slowly and with grace. You must hold your tongue when I speak. You may not shout or laugh – that is not appropriate behaviour. You have beautiful dresses and precious jewels and gilded chambers. I do not understand why you are not happy. Why can you not be satisfied?

The Prince's words echoed in Lumikki's ears. She felt it become harder to breathe. The corset squeezed her lungs shut. The edges of her vision began to quiver and darken.

'Just a little tighter and maybe you'll fall back into your eternal sleep and I can return you to your glass coffin. You were more beautiful to look at there. You were better and easier. I fell in love with the maiden in the glass box, not this unruly, impudent, misbehaving person who is all too normal and real,' the Prince whispered into Lumikki's ear.

She couldn't breathe.

Her oxygen was running out.

Lumikki tried to gasp for breath. It didn't work. She simply couldn't get her lungs full of air. The sensation of drowning. The sensation of passing out. Darkness spreading its wings before her eyes.

Lumikki collapsed, her head thumping on the floor. As her eyes swept across the stage floor, she suddenly remembered where she had seen the chest the key would fit. It was in her parents' bedroom, under the bed, wrapped in a cloth. She had seen it there, years ago, when she had been in their room getting a thermometer and it had fallen on the floor and rolled under the bed. Lumikki had wondered what the object wrapped in the dark felt could be. Peeking under the fabric, she had seen a wooden chest.

For a fleeting moment she had thought she remembered something from her childhood about treasures, but then her mum and dad had come home and Lumikki had bolted from the room as if she had been doing something forbidden. She had never asked about the chest. Of course not. She had understood that this secret was none of her business.

But now it was. Because she had the key.

That was Lumikki's final thought before she lost consciousness.

Droplets of water on her face. Like summer rain. Opening her eyes, Lumikki saw Sampsa's worried gaze.

'I'm fine,' Lumikki managed to say.

That was a lie, but in a different way than Sampsa would have understood. Lumikki lay on a soft surface, probably a blanket from the prop closet, and her feet were elevated.

Her corset had been removed. In addition to Sampsa, next to her also stood Aleksi and Tinka, who was holding a water bottle. Apparently she had been the one sprinkling water on Lumikki's face.

'I said be careful with the corset,' Tinka snapped at Aleksi.

'I didn't even make it that tight,' Aleksi said in his defence.

'It wasn't because of that,' Lumikki said and crawled to her feet. Her head threatened to go black again, but she refused to give the dizziness power over her. She had to convince the others that everything was OK, because otherwise they weren't going to let her leave.

'I probably just didn't eat enough today. And I was up late last night.'

Sampsa and Tinka glanced at each other. Aleksi looked relieved. Tinka frowned and looked at Lumikki closely.

'OK. Stuff like that happens sometimes. And you seem better now,' she finally said.

Lumikki hoped no one would notice her legs shaking. Sampsa rubbed her back with safe, calming strokes. Lumikki felt like leaning against him and letting him support her, but now was not the time for that.

'Let's wrap it up here for today,' Tinka said.

'Maybe that's a good idea,' Lumikki said. 'Since the scene is supposed to end with me getting my laces undone and running off into the forest, we went a little off script.'

She managed to make the others laugh. Good.

'Dress rehearsal in two days, then. And listen, everybody. This play is going to be fantastic! Thank you for all your hard work.'

Tinka's energy was enough to get everyone excited. Chattering voices filled the auditorium. Aleksi nudged Lumikki gently on the shoulder.

'Sorry,' he whispered.

'Don't sweat it,' Lumikki replied.

'And now I'm going to take you home and spoil you rotten,' Sampsa whispered in Lumikki's ear.

Lumikki carefully disengaged herself from his embrace.

'That sounds fantastic, but I have to go and see my parents tonight.'

Lumikki tried to look Sampsa in the eye, despite how difficult it was.

'Does it have to be tonight?' Sampsa asked.

'Well, we have this St Lucia Day tradition in our family.' Lie number two. Or, in a way, it wasn't.

Even though her father had said they weren't going to celebrate the holiday, one of his cousins had been organising parties on St Lucia Day in Turku for the past few years. Lumikki knew her dad and mum would be there today and wouldn't come home until tomorrow morning. She would have all the time she wanted to inspect the contents of the chest.

Sampsa looked disappointed. Enduring his crestfallen and still slightly concerned gaze was hard for Lumikki. But she didn't have any choice. She had to get some answers tonight or she was going to go insane.

As their lips touched, she tried not to think that it was a Judas kiss.

13

Being at home without her parents knowing felt wrong. Her footsteps echoed strangely.

The wrong girl in the wrong house, the echoes whispered. *A ghost girl who shouldn't be sneaking around these rooms alone.*

Of course her mum and dad would have given permission to come if Lumikki had asked, but she hadn't wanted them to know. She didn't want the extra questions that would just lead to more lies. Lumikki didn't want to be the kind of person who lied to her loved ones. Her stalker had forced her into it, though, with his threats.

Lumikki hoped that when she finally uncovered the secret, this 'shadow' would leave her alone. What if the stalker was just obsessed with the fact that he knew something Lumikki didn't, and the most important thing was exposing the truth?

Lumikki silenced her inner voice, which tried to whisper that an all-consuming madness like this was unlikely to be satiated by something so simple.

Her parents' bedroom smelled just like she remembered it always smelling – lavender, fresh sheets, a slight hint of houseplant soil, her dad's aftershave and the old lace curtains that had been her grandmother's. Lumikki lifted up one corner of the floor-length bedspread and peeked underneath. The blanket she remembered was there on the floor. Lumikki crawled under the bed. It was dusty. Apparently her dad didn't vacuum as manically now as he used to when Lumikki lived at home. Good for him.

Lumikki lifted the blanket. Suddenly her heart was pounding frighteningly fast. Her hands were strangely cold and clammy. But all she found under the blanket was a regular cardboard box. Not an ornate chest. A brown cardboard box full of erotic magazines.

Lumikki pushed the box back into place and covered it. It contained secrets, but not the kind of secrets she was looking for. Her parents' sex life was absolutely none of her business and she wished she had never made even this relatively innocent discovery.

She crawled out from under the bed, coughing and brushing the dust off the knees of her jeans. Disappointment. Emptiness. Could she have remembered wrong? Had she just imagined the chest entirely? What if she had just been thinking so hard about having the key that she had convinced herself of the memory of the chest, with its lock that the key fitted?

No. That couldn't be it. Lumikki wouldn't accept that.

Where in her parents' house would someone hide a chest they didn't want anyone to find?

Lumikki searched the cupboards and closets, the living room, the hallway, the basement and the small shed in the backyard. No chest. No hint of a chest. Evening had already turned to night. Hope began to change to a grey frustration.

Think, think, she urged herself as she sat on the living-room sofa. Lumikki gently rubbed her temples, trying to ward off an incipient headache. She dug the key out of her pocket and held it in her palm.

Little key, in my hand. Tell me where your lock is hidden. Lead me to the chest I seek.

The key was just a dead weight in her hand. It didn't have any answers.

'Sometimes what you seek may be closer than you think.' Lumikki had always hated 'deep' thoughts like that. But now that was all she heard, repeated monotonously in her head. Where closer? Under her rear end? Right.

Before Lumikki had even managed to think her sarcastic retort, she was tearing the cushions off the seat and opening the sofabed.

And finding the chest.

The bed part of the sofa was under the cushions, folded into a space you had to pull it from. Inside the sofa, between the bed frame and the floor, was a small space just big enough to fit a flat box for storing sheets and a blanket. But now there was the familiar wooden chest. Lumikki lifted it out with sweaty hands. She didn't waste any time admiring the decorations on the outside. The contents were the important thing. She could barely hold the key. It turned laboriously in the lock. Lumikki had to work to get the lock to finally open.

She didn't know what she had expected. She couldn't say what she believed or hoped she would find in the chest. Suddenly Lumikki had before her a childhood she never remembered having.

Photographs of a blonde, grey-eyed girl who resembled her, but not quite. Who resembled her father and mother, but not quite. Rosa Rosa Rosa Rosa. Her sister Rosa. When Lumikki saw the pictures, she suddenly remembered how her sister smelled and how she breathed in her sleep and how her arms hugged Lumikki and sometimes pinched a little, too. Rosa's giggly laugh. Her furious tantrums. Her singing and whistling that sounded like a nightingale.

Pictures of two girls together. One was shorter, with brown hair. Lumikki. They sat side by side. They waded in a lake. They ran. They danced under a sprinkler.

Lumikki wasn't looking at the pictures any more.

All her senses were suddenly awash with memories.

Strawberries in summer. Rosa gave her the biggest, reddest ones. Grandma's attic always smelled of autumn, even in summer. Grandma's old shoes, which were too big for them. They both put one foot in the same shoe. It was impossible to walk without falling. Rosa's hair tangled easily. Lumikki's didn't. Rosa brushed her hair with a hundred strokes and then another hundred. Rain was lashing the window and they built a fort under a blanket that was oranger than orange. When a scary part came in their favourite television show, Rosa put her hands over Lumikki's eyes and whispered that it was only a story. The smell of the rose bushes made them giddy, but the thorns pricked. Adults never understood the best games. Sometimes you had to get the whole floor wet in your room. Because it was the ocean. Rosa's cheeks were salty because she had been crying. Lumikki licked the salt off. She was a cat. They held each other's hands and were never going to be apart. They would always move to the same house and always sleep in the same room. They would be Snow White and Rose Red. And if they had bad dreams, they would sleep in the same bed. Warm side by warm side. Breathing in unison. Nightmares could never get in if they slept right against each other.

Lumikki didn't know how long had passed when she finally realised she was eighteen years old and was sitting on the floor of her parents' living room surrounded by photographs. Dozens and dozens of photographs scattered all around. They filled the floor, as if a new sky had opened up above her and colourful, rectangular snowflakes had fallen from it. Lumikki wasn't three any more. She wasn't holding her older sister Rosa's hand.

Lumikki felt as if a tidal wave had washed over her, stripping away the ceiling, floor and walls. The floodwater had thrust her into the middle of a black nothingness. There was no safety anywhere, no firm foundation. Everything she had believed was a lie, a black darkness. She had lived her entire life up until now believing that she was an only child, alone.

How could a sister be taken away from a person? How could they have hidden from her that Rosa ever even existed? And why? What had happened to her?

Lumikki stood up. She had to support herself on the edge of the sofa so as not to fall. She felt faint. She felt like vomiting. She felt like crying. Her feet wouldn't carry her weight. She fumbled around on the living-room table for her phone. She had to call her mum and dad right now. It didn't matter what time it was. It didn't matter if they were already sleeping. Liars. Deceivers. You couldn't do things like this to someone you loved. Could you? How could they have concealed something this big from her all her life?

Lumikki had to ask.

Now.

She had to know what had happened to Rosa.

Just then a series of text messages showed up. Lumikki guessed who they were from before she even read them.

I see you. You're standing with your phone in your hand. But don't make that call.

You don't want to perform your leading role on opening night to blood spattered on the walls. Blood running across the stage. Enough blood to fill every seat. You don't want your nice but stupid boyfriend falling and staring with lifeless eyes in the middle of his lines.

And you know cancelling the show won't help anything. I will still find all of you and act out my script. You are beautiful right now. A person who has seen the truth is always beautiful.

Lumikki rushed to turn off the living-room lights, even though she knew it wouldn't help anything.

Then she stood stock-still in the dark room and stared into the yard, trying to see something. Only blackness gazed back.

Lumikki let the hand holding her phone fall and hang limply at her side. She knew she couldn't make the call.

Knowledge is beautiful and cruel, my dear Lumikki. With knowledge you can do anything. Knowledge leads to action and belief and trust. It gives us true power.

If you know the right people, you can always get more information and find exactly what you're looking for. I know so much about you because I wanted to know. In my thirst for knowledge I was like a person who has never had a proper drink. I knew how to put the right questions to the right people. I found ways to get at everything everyone was trying to keep secret.

Nothing is secret when you're as thirsty for knowledge as me.

People are always ready to make an exception once you convince them they have a reason to share. Sometimes that takes money and sometimes other forms of payment. Usually cash isn't necessary, though, because people want to tell what they know, even their most sensitive secrets. It's in people's blood.

I've been patient collecting information about you, piece by piece. I didn't rush. I knew I had time, and when the time was right you would be ready to accept what I'd found.

Knowledge is power.
Truth is beauty.
I will make you more powerful and more beautiful than anyone else.

THURSDAY, 14 DECEMBER

14

Always walk in the light, Lumikki.

Those were Lumikki's grandmother's final words to her. Pancreatic cancer had taken her Grammy five years before. Lumikki had visited Grammy in the hospital and leaned in close so she could stroke Lumikki's cheek with her dry, wrinkled hand. Grammy had been widowed at a young age, left to raise four children on her own. Lumikki had loved Grammy, this strong yet fragile woman, without question or reserve. Grammy had loved her, too. Lumikki never doubted that for a second. Her father's parents were more distant, though. They lived in Åland, and Lumikki saw them less frequently.

But how could even Grammy have hidden from Lumikki that she had a sister? Lumikki felt as if she had been thrust into a strange artificial reality where everyone else was in a conspiracy against her. *Candid Camera.* A giant play. A reality TV show that was actually scripted, but Lumikki was the only one who didn't know.

Always walk in the light.

Her grandmother's words came to Lumikki's mind as she walked past the central square downtown on her way home from school. The patterns of the Christmas lights bathed the whole street in yellow and gold brilliance. The flower and snowflake shapes, the strands of lights wrapped around tree trunks and branches and the window displays in the shops made you forget that if the city ever suddenly lost electricity, people would have to wander around in complete and utter darkness. When there was enough light, you forgot the darkness. Lumikki wondered if her Grammy thought that, too. That if she just made Lumikki's life full enough of light and joy, the tragedy of the past would disappear.

Because there had to be a tragedy in her past. Lumikki understood that now after seeing the pictures. Only a major tragedy could offer even a partial explanation for the inconceivable fact that her sister had been hidden from her.

Lumikki hadn't slept a minute the previous night. After her stalker's text messages, she had turned off all the lights, closed all the curtains, found the sharpest knife in the kitchen and curled up in the corner of the sofa staring straight ahead. She had listened more carefully than ever before in her life and jumped at every howl of the wind, every creak of the house – even the patter of the sleet against the windows. She had been so afraid she thought she might die of it. Lumikki wanted to call Sampsa or Blaze or her parents or the police, but she couldn't.

The stalker had tied her hands and paralysed her, taking away any room to move or breathe.

As the night slowly dragged on, Lumikki had tried to think who her stalker could be, but she failed to come up with even a vaguely possible answer. A lunatic. A madman. But who could know so much? Who could know about the chest and the pictures and the key? Who could have got their hands on the key? Lumikki's parents, of course, but although she had increasingly begun to doubt their love for her, she still couldn't believe that they could be behind this kind of harassment. Her own mother and father? No, that wasn't possible.

But Lumikki wasn't really able to give her full attention to the identity of her stalker, since she was so consumed by the question of what had happened to Rosa. That felt more important than anything else. She had to get an answer to that before she could think about the rest.

The stalker had given her the key, but he'd left the larger lock shut. Lumikki knew she was at his mercy. She was sure her stalker had the answer.

When morning had finally cast its tired, grey December gaze over the northern hemisphere, Lumikki had crawled off the sofa, arms and legs numb, and on the verge of passing out. She had taken the knife back into the kitchen and then erased every trace that she had been in the house. She had completed each motion mechanically. Sometimes you had to run on autopilot when you lacked the strength and resources for anything else.

Just do what you have to. Shut out everything else.

So Lumikki had taken a morning train to Tampere, stopped by her apartment to change and drink a quick cup of coffee, and then walked to school. Normal things, normal life, as if everything was just as usual. All around people were living their lives, hurrying to work and school. Lumikki felt as if she were watching them through glass, from her glass coffin. Present, but not really there.

Once upon a time there was a girl who wasn't.

Rosa, who had just been wiped away. Lumikki, who walked and breathed and must have looked like a perfectly living person, even though all she felt inside was blackness. Just a shell of a person.

At school the first person Lumikki had encountered was Henrik Virta, her psychology teacher, who looked at her with concern.

'You aren't sick, are you?' he had asked.

'No. Just winter blues,' Lumikki had replied.

'At this time of year you have to make sure you get enough sleep and light,' Henrik had said, smiling warmly.

Lumikki had only had the energy to nod. Next she had seen Sampsa, who was even more worried about how exhausted she seemed.

'I just stayed up late with my parents,' Lumikki had lied. She had started to feel like telling one more lie might make her vomit.

'Crazy Finland-Swede party animals,' Sampsa had said with a laugh.

Somehow that had led to the fight. Lumikki was irritated by what Sampsa had said, and his smile and his tone of voice and everything, really. It made her mad when Sampsa said he would wait for her in the library after school so they could walk home to her place together.

'I'm so tired all I want to do after school is take my crazy Finland-Swede nap alone in my crazy Finland-Swede apartment,' Lumikki had said.

'I promise to be quiet and not bother you,' Sampsa had replied calmly.

'No. I want to be alone tonight.'

'You want to be alone a lot lately.'

'That's just how I am. You knew that when you started dating me.'

'Sometimes I feel like I'm a pretty insignificant part of your life.'

Lumikki had seen the sadness in Sampsa's gaze and under different circumstances it would have hurt her. But not today. She was so tired and anxious and felt so weighed down that Sampsa's sorrow only felt accusatory.

What could Lumikki have said?

I don't want you with me because every word I say to you is a lie. I'm lying to you to protect you, but today I can't do it any more. You can't save me. No one can.

She had gone through the whole school day in an impenetrable black fog. Now she was crossing the bridge over the river rapids in the centre of the city with an honour guard of horses made of light. Lumikki had always thought this was the best part of the city's Christmas lights. Rearing horses with front hooves pawing the air, their proud neighing almost audible.

Always walk in the light.

She would never get out of the blackness until she knew.

Lumikki decided that it was time to contact her stalker herself for the first time. Pulling her phone out of her pocket, she sent a text message to the number the stalker was using.

I want to meet you.

Lumikki hoped that would be a strong enough invitation for her shadow. If she had learned anything about her stalker's mind, she believed he wouldn't be able to resist the temptation.

Lumikki knew she was playing a dangerous game, but she had to find out who was behind this.

A surprise was waiting for Lumikki at her door. Sampsa. He was sitting on the stairs with a picnic basket next to him.

'If you want, I'll leave. But I thought it might do you good to have a little food and maybe a neck rub.'

Sampsa looked so disarming and sweet in his big light-green toque, with his eyes full of hope, that Lumikki thought her heart would break. What had she done to deserve such unselfish, unshakeable love?

'Did you really think you were going to take me on a picnic in December?' Lumikki asked.

'Of course. I have a blanket and everything. Your apartment is small, but there's plenty of space on the floor.'

Sampsa grinned. Grabbing the boy's coat collar, Lumikki kissed him long and tenderly, because right now Sampsa deserved that more than anyone else in the world.

Inside Sampsa really did spread the blanket out on the floor and then proceeded to produce baguettes, fresh cheeses, grapes and chocolate muffins. He put on an album of modern folk chants by Sanna Kurki-Suonio called *Black*. Sampsa sat Lumikki down, offered her bread with cheese, poured her a glass of red wine and put his hands on her shoulders.

'Now you just enjoy,' he whispered in Lumikki's ear. Lumikki

closed her eyes. Sampsa was so good and so nice that Lumikki
was afraid she would burst into tears.

I know, I know the wind and the calm.
Far shores, far shores of shadow I see.
Where shall, where shall I go here alone,
where shall, where shall I look for my rest?
I can't, I can't squeeze into the earth,
save sickness, save sickness strike at me first.
Into swamp, into swamp I shall not slip,
without death, without death's touch on my lips.
I'd sleep, I'd sleep but life wearies me not
and drink, I'd drink but I have no thirst.

The rhythm and words of the song, Sampsa's gentle touch, the
warmth of the red wine in her veins. All of it together formed a
soft, fluffy fairy-tale world around Lumikki. What if she could
just stay here? What if she could just forget everything else?
Even for a moment?

Sampsa's massage was pleasant. But Lumikki couldn't help
thinking of the other hands that made her skin feel electric in an
entirely different way, sending shocks of pleasure through her
whole body with only a few, light strokes. Blaze. She thought
of Blaze even though Blaze was precisely the one she shouldn't
be thinking about. That was unfair to Sampsa.

Just then Lumikki's phone dinged with a text message. She
reached for it.

'Don't look at it now,' Sampsa begged.

'I have to,' Lumikki replied and grabbed the phone.

Sampsa's hands slid off her shoulders. The fluffy clouds had dissipated already anyway, and Lumikki's heart was pounding in her ears, from horror and hope equally. But the text message wasn't from the stalker. It was from Blaze.

I think about you all the time. First thing in the morning and last thing at night. And all the time in between. I still love you. I will always love you.

Lumikki felt her cheeks flush. Could they really have such a strong connection that when she thought of Blaze he sensed it? Lumikki stood up. She walked into the kitchen.

'Who was it from?' Sampsa asked.

'My mum. I accidentally left a shirt at their house.' *Lie, lie, lie, lie. Another lie.*

Automatically Lumikki had opened the kitchen drawer where she kept the dragon brooch Blaze had given her and picked it up. Her fingers stroked the intricate scales. Oh if only Lumikki could have pinned it to the collar of her coat and worn it proudly. Why couldn't her life be that simple?

Lumikki heard Sampsa get up from the blanket. She quickly slipped the brooch into her pocket. Then she deleted the text message from Blaze. What she really should have done was delete his number from her phone entirely. Lumikki couldn't do that yet, though.

Come my friend
lead me to a place
that is visited by vipers and scorpions.

116

Come my friend
lead me to a place
where we will be torn into shreds by thorns.
Come my friend
lead me astray
because that's where I want to go, straight astray.

Sanna Kurki-Suonio's voice filled Lumikki's mind.

'Can we turn the music off?' she asked Sampsa.

'Of course. What do you want to do?'

'Sleep,' Lumikki replied, without looking Sampsa in the eye as she walked to the bed.

Suddenly she was so tired she couldn't stay upright. Lumikki threw herself on the bed with her clothes on, wrapped a blanket around herself and fell asleep instantly.

Lumikki didn't immediately realise what had woken her up. She glanced next to her. Sampsa was lying sound asleep. Lumikki leaned up on her elbows and looked around. Sampsa had cleaned up the picnic and folded the blanket. Lumikki had been sleeping so deeply that she hadn't heard a thing.

Not until she looked at her phone to check the time did she realise a text message had woken her up. It was 10:15 p.m. This time the message was from the stalker.

Come to Särkänniemi. What better place than an amusement park for us to meet? I'll tell you everything there.

Often I watch you, even when I can't actually see you. I have a special place just for that. I have pictures of you. I took them secretly. In the pictures you are so sweet and contemplative, since you thought no one could see you. I hung the pictures on the walls of my secret room. Sometimes I stroke your forehead with a finger. I touch the curve of your full lower lip and think about what it would be like to kiss you.

I also have all the newspaper articles about you. And a lot of papers you don't even know exist yet. I made a timeline of your life on one wall. So much has happened to you.

Did you think you'd lost that orange mitten of yours? I have it. That and your silver pen and the button that fell off your white blouse. They are the small treasures I caress, since I can't caress you yet.

Sometimes I come to my 'Lumikki room' with candles and talk to you. I watch as the glow of the flames makes your cheeks redden in the photographs. You are so beautiful. You are the most beautiful thing I know.

Pictures aren't enough, though. Mementos are just substitutes. I want you completely, with all my senses. I want to see you, to smell you, to taste you, to touch you. I have never wanted anything or anyone this much. You are the purpose of my life and the meaning of my existence, my dear Lumikki.

15

Lumikki climbed over the fence of the amusement park, hoping she wasn't going to set off some sort of alarm. The temperature had dropped below freezing and the fence was icy. However, she managed to get over to the other side without any sirens going off. Frost glittered on everything like a layer of magic dust. The otherwise empty, quiet amusement park looked eerie and threatening. The dark rides rose into the night like sleeping monsters with many arms. They were motionless but seemed as if at any moment they could tear themselves loose from the ground and start walking. The swing carousel looked like it could start spinning wildly and the chains of the chairs could snap, sending them flying in every direction. The Magic Carpet could well take flight and land in the lake, sinking gurgling under the waves.

The rides had been abandoned for the winter, left to hibernate. There was no call to wake them because they would be angry.

Lumikki had managed to slip away again without Sampsa waking up. The boy had a gift for deep sleep. This time Lumikki had left so quickly that she hadn't even left a note. She couldn't take the risk of waking him. Lumikki had to meet this 'shadow'. She had to get answers.

Now she was inside the amusement park, but she saw no sign of the stalker. Lumikki was tired of all this hiding.

'I'm here!' she yelled as loud as her lungs would allow.

The echo reverberated off the walls of the rides. No one answered.

Come to the fun house.

A text message again. Why was this stalker still giving her the run-around? She had already come here. She was ready to meet.

The door to the fun house was open. Lumikki called out a hello inside. There was no reply. She stepped in. A tilting floor, a rope bridge, a ball pit and a hall of mirrors that made you look tall or short, fat or as thin as a rake. Lumikki had been here before. She could run through it quickly. Even the blackout hall and the glass labyrinth. And the slides at the end.

Next text message.

Good. Now you've been through the strange stage we call childhood. It is skewed and distorted. You can't always trust your memories. Mirrors lie. Now it's time for you to move on to the Tornado.

Lumikki was growing frustrated and losing hope. She wanted to put an end to this. But maybe this really was the last leg of her journey. Maybe she would get her answers once she had completed these tasks.

The Tornado was the park's wildest ride, a roller-coaster with insane corkscrews. Riders sped along suspended beneath the track, sometimes upside down. The Tornado also had an enormous loop that swung all the way around.

Next instruction.

Climb along the track.

This stalker had to be completely out of his mind. Only a crazy person would go climbing on a roller-coaster track. But the real crazy person was Lumikki, because she did as she was told.

Climbing along the icy track was difficult. The metal surface was slick, making it hard to get a grip. Lumikki managed to crawl along the first few yards of flat track, but as soon as the slope steepened, climbing became almost impossible. Lumikki's strength was nearly gone already. She crept along the track on her hands and knees, hanging when it twisted and turned sharply, holding on with her legs with a vice-like grip. Sometimes she pulled herself up using only her arms. Lumikki clenched her teeth, unwilling to give in. She made the mistake of looking down. She was high up. Too high up. How high did the stalker want her to go? Lumikki closed her eyes and tried to breathe. The frigid wind lashed her cheeks. This was mad. She could fall and die at any second. Suddenly someone yelled from below.

'Lumikki!'

Lumikki would have recognised that voice anywhere. But she couldn't believe she had heard right. She glanced down again. Yes, she had heard right. Blaze.

'Come down from there! Carefully!'

Suddenly Lumikki had lost all feeling in her arms, her legs, her cheeks and her heart. Blaze. The person she loved most in all the world. The person she wanted most in all the world to trust, despite it all. Was Blaze . . .? Could he be . . .? Lumikki couldn't think the thought through to its logical conclusion. But what other explanation could there be?

But then she heard another voice. Almost as familiar.

'What the hell are you doing? Come down before I call the fire department!'

Sampsa.

Lumikki didn't understand anything any more. How could Sampsa and Blaze both be here? Her strength flagged even more. Lumikki decided to start climbing down. It was even more difficult than climbing up. Lumikki felt her grip on the metal surface failing. She wrapped her legs around the metal tube that formed the rail of the twisting track, but they slipped, leaving her hanging by her arms.

Lumikki felt her strength flag, and then she fell.

But Sampsa and Blaze had made it underneath to catch her. For a moment Lumikki was in both of their embraces, both sets of arms protectively encircling her. Protecting or imprisoning. Lumikki didn't know which any more. She extricated herself from their arms and took a few steps back.

'What the hell are you two doing here?' she asked.

'We could ask you the same thing,' Blaze replied confrontationally.

'I asked first, so you answer first.' Lumikki did not avoid Blaze's gaze.

Blaze turned his head away.

'OK. I was hanging around outside your apartment because I couldn't sleep. I guess I was hoping I might catch a glimpse of you or something, maybe in the window,' Blaze admitted. 'And when I saw you go out, I decided to follow you.'

He sounded like he was telling the truth. But Lumikki wasn't sure she could trust anyone any more. She shifted her gaze to Sampsa.

'And you?'

'I read the text you got. It didn't wake you up right away. And when you woke up, I pretended to be asleep and then followed you. For a long time I've been feeling like you must be seeing someone else.'

At first Sampsa looked ashamed, but then he raised his jaw defiantly.

'And apparently I was right. You came here to meet *him*.'

Sampsa emphasised the last word with disdain and nodded towards Blaze.

'No, I didn't,' Lumikki said.

'Well, then why?'

Lumikki didn't answer. She was so confused. Was Blaze telling the truth? Was Sampsa telling the truth? Was neither of them the stalker? Or could they both be in it together? Was this a conspiracy?

'Whatever happened, it's pretty clear you aren't needed here any more,' Blaze said to Sampsa.

Turning to Blaze, Sampsa stepped too close to him, invading his personal space.

'I'd like to remind you that Lumikki is my girlfriend,' Sampsa said.

125

'Who kissed me only a couple of days ago.'

Sampsa looked to Lumikki as if asking her to deny this.

Again Lumikki didn't reply, but her eyes said enough. Sampsa shoved Blaze.

'Get out of our life!' he snapped. 'You already left Lumikki once. You missed your chance.'

Blaze gave a crooked smile and pushed Sampsa back gently, almost playfully.

'True love doesn't care about things like that. Lumikki and I belong together. It's fate.'

'You talk pretty big considering you weren't man enough to stand by Lumikki's side,' Sampsa spat.

'Oh, so now we're going to see who's the real man?'

Suddenly Blaze and Sampsa were grappling with each other. Both growled curses even as they shouted to one another that Lumikki really loved them. Dead tired, Lumikki watched the display, again as if through glass. She didn't cheer either of them on or wish that either one would lose. The fight just looked stupid. Juvenile.

'I can't handle this right now,' Lumikki sighed. 'You two can stay here and beat each other to a bloody pulp for all I care. I'm leaving. And don't bother following me.'

Then Lumikki took off running without a backwards glance. She wanted to feel her exhausted muscles strained even further. She wanted the frozen air to torture her lungs. Lumikki wanted something, anything that would clear the fog of uncertainty from her mind.

Could a person go crazy without knowing it? Or was that the normal way of going crazy? What if she really had lost her grip on reality? What if she had just imagined it all? What if the letters had never existed? Or the text messages? Or the stalker?

What if it had all just been in Lumikki's head?

Lumikki jumped at the fence, grabbed it with her fingers and the tips of her shoes and climbed over. She continued running. As she reached the main road that ran along the shore of the lake, someone shouted after her.

'Hey, baby! The party's just getting started!'

A group of middle-aged men, apparently just leaving a Christmas party at the marina. At least, that's what the elf hats and red noses suggested. Lumikki just kept on running. She would have liked to run away from everything, away from her life, away from the madness that her days had turned into.

She still didn't have any answers. She still didn't know who was stalking her.

When Lumikki opened her apartment door, she felt like collapsing on the floor and crying. How much could a person endure? How much did she have to carry on her own? Where was the line when a person just broke?

Lumikki was in such a state of confusion and distress that she realised too late there was a smell that didn't belong. By the time she realised, her hands were already twisted behind her back in a tight grip, a leather glove was shoved into her mouth and her sleeve was pulled up.

The last thing Lumikki was aware of was the sharp point of a needle pressing against her bare arm and something being injected into her vein.

Then the world was replaced by blackness.

FRIDAY, 15 DECEMBER,
EARLY MORNING

16

The shadow hovered sometimes closer and sometimes further off. Its silhouette was indistinct and shifting. She couldn't quite make out its shape.

Lumikki tried to focus. Everything was so blurry. Her head ached and her arms and legs felt heavy, like in a nightmare. Her eyelids wanted nothing but to fall shut again. She forced them open, though.

Lumikki was lying on her back. She moved her left hand away from her body and it struck an obstacle. The same thing happened with her right. And both legs. She just managed to lift one of her hands up far enough to discover a barrier there, too. Strange. She could still see up and to the sides. Or she would have been able to if everything weren't so clouded. Clouded eyes, clouded thoughts, which she also couldn't seem to focus.

'And it wasn't long before she opened her eyes.'

The voice came from above Lumikki. It came from the shadow that moved. Lumikki had the vague realisation that the voice was familiar, but she couldn't put her finger on it.

'I knew you would be stronger than the Princess in the story. No poison could affect you for very long. You're a fighter.

You've been fighting your entire life. You've fought against me valiantly, too. You didn't show your fear. You didn't tell anyone.'

The fog began to clear a little from Lumikki's head. Finally she realised what was preventing the slow, laboured movements of her arms and legs. She was in a casket. In the glass coffin from the play.

'But now your struggle is over,' the shadow's voice continued. 'You don't have to fight any more. You can give in now and be mine.'

Lumikki tried to sit up. She felt as if her veins had been poured full of black lead, which prevented her from moving normally. Her head banged against the glass top of the coffin. She struggled, managed to lift up her hands and tried to push the cover off.

It should have been easy. She knew that. She had done it time and time again in rehearsal. Now the cover didn't budge.

'Poor little Lumikki. Sometimes life gives us surprises. Everything doesn't go the way we thought. Sometimes you can't get out of a glass coffin so easily. This isn't a play. This isn't a fairy tale. This is real. And in reality, of course, the glass coffin's lid is screwed shut.'

Lumikki tried to make her fumbling mind recognise the voice. It was so familiar. She should have known. She should have been able to think of the name.

The name was so familiar.

She had said it so many times.

She just couldn't find it in the haze that shrouded her brain. But she knew the voice wasn't lying now. The lid really was screwed shut.

'What it may surprise you to know is that a glass coffin screwed shut is completely airtight. So you should be sparing with your breath. The oxygen won't last forever. And I'm sure you want to be conscious the whole time I'm telling you everything I know about you.'

Lumikki lay back down. *Relax*, she ordered herself. *Only breathe as much as you have to. Stay calm. Otherwise you're never going to survive this.*

You're never going to survive this.

Terror crept along Lumikki's neck as she heard those words in her mind. They could easily be true.

'I'm sure you've read all of my letters, so you're well acquainted with how much I know about you. I've been studying you for quite some time. I've followed you and watched you, guarded you and protected you, spied on you and followed your steps. I've done this because early on a feeling came to me that we two are the same. There is a darkness that lives in us.'

Lumikki felt like vomiting. She wasn't sure whether the nausea was a result of the words the voice was saying or whatever she had obviously been drugged with. She tried to breathe more evenly. To bring her heart rate closer to resting.

'You may have balked at all my talk of blood and killing. I've seen your expression once or twice when you were reading my letters. You looked shocked and afraid. Needlessly. I never would have written those things to you if I didn't know you were a killer, too. Actually, of the two of us, only you are a killer. I just enjoy the idea of killing. I suppose it's unavoidable that eventually I'll carry out my fantasy. That hasn't happened

133

yet, though. If you had been stupider and told someone about my letters and messages, I would have carried out my threats. It would have given me a reason and a justification. What is your reason and justification, my love? Just the desire to kill? An innate evil? Not to worry, though. Either option is just as stimulating for me.'

The shadow circled the glass coffin like a predator his prey. Considering how to strike and at what moment. Would he sink his teeth first into the thigh or the arm or the throat?

'I don't know whether you're just a good actor or if you really don't remember. I suppose your memories would have started coming back, at least when you read my letters. Your bloody hands. How you killed your sister Rosa.'

Lumikki's pulse shot up to panic level. Could this shadow really know? Was it true? Had she really killed her sister?

'Oh my dear Lumikki, how pale you look. Perhaps you don't remember. How you plunged the sharp knife into your sister's stomach and stood coldly by, watching as she bled out. You didn't call the babysitter for help. She arrived when it was already too late. I've read all of the police reports.'

Lumikki's clouded thoughts and senses completely lost their focus on the present. However, the shadow's words suddenly made her remember the past perfectly. Closing her eyes, she was three years old.

Lumikki was three and Rosa was six. Mum and Dad were away somewhere, probably at the theatre, and their babysitter was a bored teenage girl from next door, Jennika. That night Jennika was having a fight with her boyfriend, which she was thrashing out on the phone, repeatedly calling the boy, her own friends and the boy's friends. All Lumikki and Rosa got to eat for dinner were barely reheated leftover pancakes and strawberry jam.

'So why do you get to suck face with whoever you want, but I'm a whore if I just talk to a guy?' Jennika snapped angrily into the phone, this time to her boyfriend.

'What's a whore?' Lumikki asked.

'It's a girl with lots of boyfriends,' Rosa replied with the assurance of a big sister.

Jennika glanced at them wearily.

'Take care of your sister,' Jennika told Rosa, pointing at Lumikki. 'Try not to kill each other for a few minutes.'

Then Jennika went upstairs so she could talk in peace.

There was too much strawberry jam for the small pancakes, so the plates were covered with it.

'Let's play death!' Rosa suggested.

'How do we play that?' Lumikki asked.

'Like this,' Rosa explained and rubbed strawberry jam on the front of her white nightshirt. 'This is blood.'

Lumikki did the same. The jam was slippery and it dripped on the floor. Her hands got sticky. Lumikki laughed. Rosa wasn't satisfied yet, though.

'There has to be a weapon for blood to come out, though,' she said, walking to a drawer.

Lumikki was startled to see a sharp knife in Rosa's hand.

'We're not allowed to touch the knives,' she whispered.

'Mum and Dad aren't here, though. And besides, this is just a game,' Rosa said.

'OK,' Lumikki whispered uncertainly.

'I'm so sad. I just want to die,' Rosa explained.

'Why?'

'Maybe my boyfriend just left me. I don't want to live any more!' Rosa lamented in a dramatic voice, waving the knife in the air. 'I'm going to kill myself!' Then she pointed the tip of the knife towards her stomach. In the air, of course, a safe distance from her nightshirt.

After that everything happened quickly. Rosa slipped on the jam on the floor. She fell forwards, holding the knife, which sank into her stomach. Collapsing on her face on the floor, she didn't get up. Lumikki ran to her sister's side and nudged her shoulder. Rosa did not react. Blood began pooling under her.

'This is a stupid game,' Lumikki said. Rosa didn't answer.

'Talk to me!' Lumikki demanded, shoving Rosa over on her back with all her strength.

Her sister's eyes were open, but they didn't look at Lumikki. Blood trickled from her mouth.

Lumikki realised that something was very wrong.

She ran and ran and ran upstairs. She screamed for Jennika. Jennika was in the bathroom. She was crying and yelling.

'I've never loved anyone as much as I love you!'

Lumikki pounded on the bathroom door.

'What is it now?' Jennika snapped through the door.

'Rosa. Rosa. It's a stupid game.'

'Well, tell her you want to play something else. Leave me alone for a few seconds now, will you?' Jennika said in a tearful voice.

Lumikki was crying, too, but no tears were coming out.

She ran to the medicine cabinet in her parents' bedroom and took out a box of plasters. If you're bleeding, you need a plaster. She grabbed the ones with Mickey Mouse on them. Rosa liked those.

Then she ran back downstairs. Rosa was still lying on the floor. There was so much red blood. The knife was sticking out of her stomach. It looked wrong. A knife wasn't supposed to be like that. Lumikki tried to take it out, but she failed. She put plasters around the knife, but they instantly soaked with blood. Rosa's white nightshirt was all bloody. The plasters didn't help. The hurtie didn't go away.

The blood was sticky like strawberry jam, but it was warm, not cold.

Finally a red-eyed Jennika came down sniffling. She stopped in the doorway to the kitchen.

'What the hell . . .?'

'We were playing death,' Lumikki said. 'But it's a stupid game. I don't like it.'

Lumikki knew the memory was true. She hadn't imagined it and it wasn't a result of the drug. That was how it had all happened. And the memory explained every one of the strange flashbacks and nightmares Lumikki had ever had. She'd had a sister who had died. But it had been an accident. She wasn't a killer.

Did her mum and dad think she was? Did they think that Lumikki had taken the knife out of the drawer and stabbed Rosa in the stomach? Was that why they had hidden her sister and everything that happened from her? Lumikki had to talk to them. Right now. She had to get out of this glass coffin.

Carefully Lumikki tested whether the weakness and heaviness in her arms and legs had faded at all. It hadn't. Breathing felt more arduous now, too. Her oxygen was running out.

'Everyone thought you were so small you couldn't understand what you did. They considered it an accident. Things like that happen sometimes when normal children are playing. But what normal child wouldn't have immediately run to get the babysitter? And according to the child psychologist, you were uncommunicative, even angry. You kept repeating how stupid Rosa was. When I read your papers, I saw deep into your soul. I saw that it is just as black as mine. As black as ebony. And that was when I began to fall in love with you.'

No, no, no.

Lumikki shook her head. It didn't go like that. Jennika lied. She remembered being surprised about it even then. She had hated Jennika for lying, and she had hated her mother and father for being away from home, and she had hated Rosa for wanting to play a game that turned out real. She had hated her sister because she had died. She had hated Rosa because she had loved her so much and because suddenly she was gone.

Lumikki tried to breathe more sparingly. She was beginning to feel the lack of oxygen as an increasing faintness and blurring of her eyes.

Was this glass coffin going to turn into her actual coffin?

Lumikki searched her clothing for anything she could use as a weapon to get out. She didn't have a belt with a buckle to use. Not even a hairpin. One hand groped in her trouser pocket. Something metal. Something cold. Something whose surface felt very familiar against her fingers. Her own, personal dragon.

It was a brooch, and brooches have pins. What if Lumikki could scratch the glass with the pin and weaken it? She squeezed her fingers around the dragon. She searched for the clasp and opened it. The pin was sharp. Slowly and carefully she brought her hand out of her pocket. The shadow was on the right-hand side of the glass coffin now. Lumikki pressed the pin against the left wall of the coffin as hard as she could and moved it down.

The thin pin gave out instantly, bending beyond any use.

Tears of fear and frustration welled in Lumikki's eyes.

She was never getting out of this coffin.

Perhaps you're wondering, why you.

Because you are special, my dear Lumikki. There is light and darkness inside of you. You aren't like all the others. You're stronger than anyone else I've seen, even though you're also so fragile and vulnerable. You aren't afraid to be alone. You know that the others aren't quite as valuable as you. There are so many facets and layers to you. You have depths at eighteen that most other people will never have.

You have experienced sorrow and hate. You aren't only good.

I knew that we would meet as equals because the same black blood runs through us. That's something no one else can understand.

When I saw you for the first time, I knew instantly. It's been years since then. You didn't know then how deeply and truly I saw you. Someone had just left me who had never been able to value my ideas and my deepest inner self. After she left I thought I might never find someone like me.

Then you came.

You came like a quiet storm. The others didn't understand your power, but I felt the wind and saw the thunderclouds and

141

the lightning and all the magnificence and beauty that only exists in the most violent storms. Riders on the storm.

That's what we are. Riders on the storm. The laws and norms of this world and society don't apply to us, because we are exceptional creatures.

I'm so happy that you will soon be mine. Only mine.

17

Lumikki felt as if her heart would stop when Florence + the Machine's 'Breath of Life' began echoing through the auditorium.

'This is your favourite, isn't it? Don't look so surprised, my dear. I said I've been following your each and every step. I know what music you listen to. And I thought this would be a good fit for this occasion. You're longing for a breath of air to save you. You need oxygen. You'll get it soon. I just have to ensure first that you really love me too and understand that we have to be together, the two of us.'

The shadow's voice had turned a little tenser. Lumikki's brain still couldn't quite get a grip on it. She couldn't put it in the right box and attach the right nametag to it.

Who was this lunatic? And what did he intend to do to Lumikki?

Lumikki knew she couldn't just wait and see. She had to do something.

Lumikki could still feel the scales of the dragon against her fingers. Holding the brooch comforted her, even though the pin was bent. She stroked the surface of the dragon's skin with her finger – its head and ears, the wings lying along its back, the tail that ended in a sharp point. So sharp that it hurt Lumikki's finger.

The tip of the tail. It was clearly stronger, more substantial than the pin.

Lumikki calmed her racing pulse. She had to stay calm. The harder her heart pounded, the more she would need oxygen. And she was out of that. Hypoxia. Oxygen deprivation. Lumikki refused to think about what would follow that and how quickly.

She pressed the tail of the dragon against the glass, strained with all her might and pulled downwards. She felt the metal bite into the glass. The dragon would leave a mark. How deep? Would it weaken the glass enough?

Lumikki knew that she would only have one chance. She had to succeed on the first try.

The brooch had left a scratch. Lumikki's hand trembled as she slipped the dragon back in her pocket. For a moment she collected all her strength. She had to hold on. Her oxygen had to last a few more seconds.

Lumikki filled her lungs with all the oxygen she could still get inside the glass coffin. Then she slammed her elbow with all her strength right against the scratch she had made. Such intense pain shot through Lumikki's elbow that her vision flashed red.

But the glass shattered. The wall of the coffin collapsed and Lumikki rolled out, shielding her face. The sharp, jagged glass tore at her clothing and arms. Tiny shards of glass penetrated her skin. Lumikki didn't care. Oxygen filled her lungs.

The shadow was at her side in a second. Lumikki had expected as much.

'I should have guessed you wouldn't wait patiently . . .' he said, bending over her.

Again with her elbow, Lumikki hit him straight in the nose, and when the shadow stood up, crying out in pain, Lumikki succeeded in lifting herself up enough to strike the shadow in the crotch with her other elbow.

It worked. The stalker bent over double.

Lumikki rolled to the edge of the stage and off. She tried to fall as softly as possible, but the hard floor still hurt. Her legs still felt like two heavy bars of lead. She knew she wouldn't be able to stand. Not yet, at least. She started dragging herself across the floor with her arms.

She had to hide somewhere, quickly. Hide. But where?

Her literature classroom was next to the auditorium. Lumikki began hauling herself that way. She covered the distance painfully slowly. Her elbows hurt. The glass shards felt like they were digging deeper into her skin.

Somewhere behind her, the shadow groaned. He would recover from her blow soon enough. Running to where she was would take no time at all.

The door to the classroom was open a crack. Lumikki could already hear the shadow moving. Lumikki pushed the door open with a hand, dragged herself inside and managed to lever herself up high enough to grab the handle and push the door shut. Immediately she felt the shadow tugging at the door handle from the other side. Lumikki clenched her teeth together in pain and with other hand stretched up to turn the lock.

Then her strength gave out and she collapsed, panting, with her back against the door.

'Oh Lumikki. My poor little Lumikki,' the shadow laughed through the door. 'Did you really think I wouldn't have a key? Of course I do. You just wait here while I get it from the locker room. Then we can chat some more.'

Again the feeling came over Lumikki that she couldn't breathe.

18

The fear of death was a wondrous thing. The survival instinct pumped Lumikki's muscles full of strength they didn't otherwise have. Suddenly Lumikki's arms and legs worked again. Her brain issued commands to her muscles so quickly that she didn't have time to clothe her strategy in thought. She just acted.

As many desks and chairs in front of the door as possible. Those would slow him down. Collect everything loose she could throw. Open the window.

The key turned in the lock.

'Help!' Lumikki shouted out of the window as loud as her lungs could manage.

She couldn't see anyone outside. But there had to be someone in the park, a dog walker or someone on their way downtown or to the library?

The door slowly opened a crack. The legs of the desks and chairs screeched along the floor as they moved.

'You've built up barriers between us, my love. I would have thought we'd be past all these worldly obstacles by now.'

The shadow grunted as he struggled to open the door. A

couple of desks and chairs fell. Their clatter echoed in the classroom and hallway.

'Help!' Lumikki screamed again.

Outside it was snowing. Light, soft, white snow. The first real, beautiful snowfall this winter.

'No one will hear you,' the shadow said.

But there was uncertainty in his voice. That gave Lumikki's lungs additional strength. The shadow pushed his way into the room but didn't turn on the light. He wanted to be in the darkness and melt into it.

But Lumikki recognised him anyway. The fog swirling in her mind parted, and Lumikki realised who her stalker was.

Henrik Virta. Her psychology teacher.

This realisation startled Lumikki. How could Henrik have so much information about her? And how could such an empathetic and friendly-seeming teacher be so insanely cruel? Lumikki didn't have time to mull these questions over in her mind, though, because Henrik was shoving the desks and chairs out of his way in a rage.

'You fucking temptress!' he yelled. 'Why did you do this to me? I only want to love you and protect you. To make you safe from everything evil. We are the same soul, you and I.'

Lumikki grabbed a stapler and threw it at Henrik with all her strength. He managed to dodge it at the last second and the stapler clattered against the wall.

'You missed,' Henrik said, satisfaction in his voice.

'Just like you missed in your psychological evaluation of me,' Lumikki couldn't help saying. 'There isn't anything alike about us. You have never known me and you never will. And that isn't love. That's just a sick obsession.'

Lumikki's fear had disappeared. It had disappeared the instant she recognised Henrik and knew that he had never seen her deepest thoughts and feelings. Lumikki's core, her heart, was outside of this man's grasp. He would never reach her.

'If I can't have you, no one else will either.'

Henrik's voice had turned quiet and low. Lumikki knew he was serious. He would kill Lumikki if he could reach her.

A hole punch. Lumikki hurled it at his head. Henrik didn't have time to dodge it and the sharp corner of the hole punch hit him in the temple. In surprise Henrik raised his hand and touched his face.

'Now blood is flowing from somewhere else besides my heart,' he whispered.

The melodrama was nauseating. It was as if Henrik believed he was in some kind of play where he had to deliver the darkest, fiercest lines he could invent.

'Help!' Lumikki shouted again, her voice now hoarse.

Henrik pushed the last desk out of his way. He would reach Lumikki in just a few strides.

'You can't get away,' he growled. 'I don't understand why you don't give in to me.'

Never, Lumikki thought and climbed onto the windowsill.

'What are you doing?'

Henrik's voice was suddenly startled.

Lumikki sat down and scooted herself to the edge of the windowsill. Then she lowered herself down, hanging from the cold edge. She glanced below. The fall was a long way. Too far. But she didn't have any other options.

'Don't be crazy!' Henrik exclaimed.

'You're the crazy one here,' Lumikki replied.

Lumikki felt Henrik's hands brush her fingertips, but by then she had already let go and was falling towards the earth with snowflakes swirling all around. She tried to relax as much as possible when she landed in the schoolyard.

As she lay on her back in the newly fallen blanket of snow, Lumikki marvelled for a moment at the fact that she hadn't broken anything. Snowflakes drifted in perfect minuets, dancing on her face and melting on her cheeks.

Then the pain came.

THURSDAY, 28 DECEMBER,
TWO WEEKS LATER

19

First, Lumikki only moved her arms. Slowly, with long, patient strokes, her elbows straight, almost to her ears and then back, almost to her ribs. The snow was fluffy and soft. It moved easily as she did. Then she remembered you were supposed to move your legs, too.

It had been so long since she had done this. Not since she was a child. Before she started school? Probably. During primary school, the bullies had dumped her in snowdrifts so many times that the thought of lying down in the snow voluntarily wasn't the slightest bit appealing.

Snow angel.

The name was beautiful, even though all it really meant was the depression her body left in the snow. Wings that the movements of her arms had formed. The gown her legs had shaped.

Snow angels. Lumikki and Rosa used to fill the yard with them. Before going to sleep, Rosa had told Lumikki a bedtime story about the flock of angels that would descend from heaven during the night to sleep in the beds they had made for them. Rosa had said she was going to stay up to see the arrival of the glowing beings. Lumikki had made her sister promise to wake her up. Rosa promised and took Lumikki by the hand. And so Lumikki slipped into sleep with Rosa's warm hand gently holding hers.

Tears ran down the side of Lumikki's face towards her ears.

More memories came every day. It was like she had a cupboard inside her full of infinite drawers. One by one the drawers were opening. All the drawers that had been locked for so many years.

Once upon a time there was a secret girl.

Once upon a time there was a girl who wasn't.

Now Rosa wasn't secret any more. And although she had died, she still existed in memories and photographs and stories people told. She was no longer erased from existence. Grasping that her sister's entire existence had been concealed from Lumikki was still difficult. It was so appalling. She would never be able to accept her parents' decision.

They had made it in a state of shock, crazy with grief and trauma. Lumikki's parents really had believed that Lumikki had killed Rosa. By accident, yes, in the course of a game. Jennika's statement supported that, and the child psychologists weren't able to get anything out of Lumikki that contradicted that version of events. Apparently Lumikki had just talked about how they were 'playing death'.

Lumikki's father and mother had thought that bearing that kind of guilt would be too great a burden for a child. That was why it was just better to shut that part of their lives away. Lumikki thought that, really, it was more a question of her parents' inability to face their past. Their daughter had been taken away. For them, it was easier to think that she had never existed. They simply rejected the truth, because they couldn't endure it.

So they created a new, single-child family. They had destroyed almost every trace of Rosa. Only the photographs still existed, stored in the girls' former treasure chest. They had moved away from Turku. They had sworn the entire extended family never to breathe a word about Rosa. A vow of silence. A family of secrets. It was incomprehensible that it had worked. At first Lumikki had asked about her sister, but when no one answered or they just said she didn't have a sister, she stopped. Her dad and mum had thought that she would forget, because children do so easily. In a way that had happened, too, for many years.

But the past can't be erased so easily. Everything leaves a mark on a person.

The whole experience surrounding the death had made her father unable to work for a while. First he had travelled alone to Prague to think about what he wanted out of his life. They had considered divorce. Lumikki was only hearing about all of this now, a decade and a half after the fact. The family's financial situation had collapsed, which was why they didn't have the money to live in as large and beautiful a house as they had in Turku. They became a family where the most important things were never said out loud. They had become the façade of a family.

CHRISTMAS EVE,
FOUR DAYS EARLIER

Lumikki sat on the sofa and looked at the mantelpiece. Now in addition to one daughter's picture there was also another of them both together. As it always should have been. Her mum brought her more mulled wine. They had just finished their Christmas dinner a little while earlier.

Her mother gently, tentatively touched Lumikki's hair. There were more words in that touch than there could have been in any long monologue. This touch was an apology for all the years when her mother hadn't known how to be a real mother.

Silent night, holy night
All is calm, all is bright
Round yon virgin, mother and child
Holy infant, tender and mild
Sleep in heavenly peace,
Sleep in heavenly peace.

Her dad hummed along with the song. Lumikki saw the tears running down his cheeks. This was the first time she had ever seen him cry. Or, at least, the first time she could remember. Maybe the time would come when at moments like this it would be natural for Lumikki to stand up, walk over to her father in his armchair and hug him long and hard. But it wasn't that time yet.

They were still a silent family. Years of not talking didn't go away in a couple of weeks. But now there was a completely different, more peaceful, honest tone to the silence. It wasn't oppressive or suffocating any more. The silence didn't stop up Lumikki's mouth and strangle her. She could breathe. She could be at rest and trust that the words would come in time.

When Lumikki fell from the window, a late dog walker had just been passing the school. He immediately called an ambulance. Lumikki was rushed to the hospital. She had come through with few injuries, just bruises and sprains, nothing broken. She was forced to wear a neck brace for a week, but that was minor.

When her father and mother came to the hospital, Lumikki told them everything. A wave of relief washed over the sterile hospital room when Lumikki's parents learned that Rosa's death really had been an accident. They contacted Jennika, who after all these years was also relieved that she could finally tell the whole truth. The lie had weighed heavily upon her.

Rosa's death had been a tragic accident, and no one was to blame. What-ifs were never going to bring her back. Understanding and accepting that helped everyone touched by the tragedy. Piece by piece, step by step, they could take the repressed past back into their lives and make it a part of themselves.

Lumikki tasted the spices in her warm mulled wine. Cinnamon, cloves, ginger. She looked at the slow, dreamy motion of the geometric straw mobile hanging from the ceiling. Outside, white snow was falling. The Christmas album they were listening to would soon be over and it would be time to go to sleep.

Lumikki believed she would sleep a long, long time, deeply, without any nightmares, in complete safety.

Lumikki continued to make the snow angel, improving the shape of the wings. She thought of Henrik.

Her shadow. Her stalker. An obsessed man, the depth of whose manic insanity had only been revealed after he was caught. When Lumikki fell from the window, Henrik had fled from the school to his home. Two hours later the police broke the door down. They found Henrik unconscious on his bed. He had taken an overdose of sleeping pills, but the hospital staff had succeeded in saving him.

At first they hadn't found anything incriminating in his apartment, but then it turned out he had indeed built himself a 'Lumikki room' in the building's attic space, by covering the chicken wire walls with cardboard so no one could see inside.

When the authorities were finally able to interrogate him, they had found that his obsession with Lumikki had begun immediately after she had started at the school. Henrik's long-term girlfriend had suddenly left him, and his mental health had collapsed. He had noticed Lumikki, who stood out from the other students, and fallen in love. Henrik had then begun collecting information about her.

He was astonishingly patient, persistent and devious. He had interviewed people who'd known Lumikki at her previous school. He had gotten wind of the bullying from some of Lumikki's old classmates. Next, he'd set about finding out the names of the bullies and the extent of the bullying. Henrik knew how to make an impression on people: he was calm, charismatic and credible. Sometimes he had posed as himself, sometimes as a reporter and sometimes as Lumikki's school counsellor or therapist. People had trusted him.

Henrik had found out who Lumikki's relatives were. At the end of a night out drinking, Lumikki's father's cousin, Mats Andersson, finally revealed that Lumikki had had an older sister who died. Using every possible skill and connection he had, Henrik had ultimately succeeded in getting his hands on the police report about Rosa's death.

There were always people who knew people. Finland was a small country. If you wanted to know something, you just had to be determined and cunning enough. Henrik's psychopathy meant that all of his intelligence and charm was relentlessly bent towards achieving his goal.

When Lumikki started dating, it had driven Henrik to action. His obsession had grown by leaps and bounds. His desire to have Lumikki as his own had had no limits, and he would stop at nothing to get her. He had wanted to know everything about Lumikki, to own her, to control her with what he knew. That was also part of Henrik's power game.

Henrik had spied on Lumikki. He had followed her. Stalked her. Henrik had tracked Lumikki's every movement. His most brazen act had been going to talk to Lumikki's parents. Telling them that he also worked as the school psychologist, he had reported that Lumikki went to see him several times to talk about her dark thoughts. Henrik had made Lumikki's parents swear not to tell her about his visit. At the same time, he had stolen the key to the picture chest, the location of which Mats Andersson had revealed.

Lumikki didn't even know everything that Henrik had done. And she didn't want to know. The most important thing was that he was in prison now and couldn't stalk her any more.

Opening night of *The Black Apple* was postponed, but the show went on, one day before Christmas break. Lumikki had wanted them to put on the play still, despite what had happened. She acted her role wearing the neck brace, and in the end the performance was better than anyone could have hoped.

It was an important night for Lumikki. It did her good to see that the images of horror Henrik had painted for her did not come to pass. They only existed in his sick imagination and would never become reality.

The snow didn't feel cold under her back. Not yet. Lumikki decided to remain lying down for a while and look at the bright, starry sky that arced over her – dark, distant and full of points of light.

She didn't believe that people turned into angels after they died. She didn't think that Rosa was somewhere out there looking down on her and watching over her life. Lumikki had a hard time thinking about the possibility that there could be life after death, at least in any form like this current one.

That thought didn't feel bad or sad. This was just how it was. Human life had a certain duration, a beginning and an end. Between which was an amazing amount of space. Every breath contained more than anyone could imagine.

Lumikki knew that if she had decided differently, she could have been lying in the snow right now hand in hand with Sampsa.

And if she had decided differently, she could have been lying in the snow right now hand in hand with Blaze.

Lumikki's hands were empty. She was alone.

She had been forced to tell Sampsa that she couldn't keep seeing him. She had really liked him and got along great with him and even loved him in a way. But Sampsa had never seen deep into her thoughts, into the shadows of her forest. Sampsa couldn't have seen those things, because for him they didn't exist. His world was different, brighter and more full of light.

Lumikki had also been forced to tell Blaze that she could never go back to him. She had loved him, and loved him still, passionately, with all her heart. Blaze saw her completely. But Blaze was also able to hurt her so deeply that Lumikki could never expose herself to that kind of danger again.

But the biggest reason why Lumikki had needed to say goodbye to both Sampsa and Blaze was that she couldn't trust either of them completely. She had thought at one point that either one of them could be her stalker – even though it was only for a fleeting moment at the amusement park, and her doubts had disappeared soon afterwards. Still, those doubts told her that she couldn't trust with all her heart. How could she be with someone she didn't trust? How could she look either of them in the eye – a person who she had imagined, even for a second, could be capable of that kind of evil and cruelty? No one should have to be with someone who had thought about them that way.

The tears continued running down her face. Lumikki let them flow freely.

She cried for many reasons all at once.

She cried for her dead sister, whom she hadn't been able to mourn for all these years.

She cried for her family, which would never have the kind of warm, intimate bonds of trust that families could have.

She cried because she had been forced to give up happiness and love.

She cried because she was alone.

The stars in the sky suddenly felt closer. The light of those distant twinkling suns was comforting. The universe was enormous. Lumikki's tears stopped flowing. Suddenly she felt better. She was so small compared to everything. In this universe everyone was alone in the end, but no one was alone. Everything was made of the same elements. Lumikki was just as strong and weak as crystals and rocks, waves and reeds, grass and rotting leaves, the burning heart of the sun and the cold void of space.

She had just as many layers and branched in just as many directions as a fairy tale a thousand years old. One that had started long before the words 'once upon a time' and which would continue long after the words 'and they lived happily ever after'. Because nothing really happened only once. All stories existed many times, morphing and changing. And no one lived happily ever after. Or unhappily. Everyone lived happily and unhappily, both at different times and sometimes both at once.

This was Lumikki's universe. In its darkness and light was room for passion and fear, despair and joy. The air that filled her lungs was heady. In the embrace of the sky she became more whole. She became more herself. She was free. Lumikki pressed her palms against the snowy ground and wished that she could become one with the freshly fallen flakes, merging with their infinitude.

A gentle night breeze blew through the park, moving the black branches of the trees and their shadows on the drifts.

The world sighed and throbbed around Lumikki as if it had one single pulse. Her pulse.